Lock Down Publications and Ca$h Presents

I0679264

SAVAGE DREAMZ

THE CIRCLE

Written By
KING DAVID

Lock Down Publications
P.O. Box 944
Stockbridge, GA 30281
www.lockdownpublications.com

Like our page on Facebook: Lock Down Publications
www.facebook.com/lockdownpublications.ldp

Stay Connected with Us!

Text **LOCKDOWN** to 22828 to stay up-to-date with new releases, sneak peaks, contests and more…

Like our page on Facebook:
Lock Down Publications

Join Lock Down Publications/The New Era Reading Group

Visit our website:
www.lockdownpublications.com

Follow us on Instagram:
Lock Down Publications

Email Us: We want to hear from you!

Chapter 1

Chauncey woke up with a startle, reaching for his fire, as loud banging noises continued coming from his living room. Instead of reaching for his pants, he grabbed his bulletproof vest, strapping it on tight, mumbling to his self, vowing, "If it's war they want, it's war they're gonna get."

Cutting off the hallway lights, he silently crept to the living room, searching for the shoes he had kicked off when coming in, in case he had to make a run for it.

One thing about it, Chauncey wasn't scary, by far, but he damn sure wasn't stupid either and knew that he couldn't take on the world by his damn self. This wasn't a movie; it was real-life shit, where bullets wouldn't just mysteriously disappear or go around you if you were standing in the direct line of fire.

Before he could finish lacing up his shoes, the front door came flying off the hinges with a loud bang. He instantly thought about Melissa still lying in the bed, as well as his money and stash hidden in the top of the closet, and said fuck both as he ran toward the back door.

Had it been one or two, maybe even three, he would have stood his ground and shot it out until his clip ran dry. But seeing five bare-faced natives running in let him know that this was more than just a simple robbery or home invasion. Plus, he knew that the seventeen he had in the clip wasn't a match against the artillery the natives were holding, especially if there were more outside.

Reaching the back door, he once again thought about Melissa lying in the bed and shook his head. Even though he had once loved her, it would be better if they killed her since he didn't get a chance. Seeing that she knew where all the bodies were buried that he'd killed over the years, he had recently started doubting her love and truthfully didn't trust her anymore, seeing how strange she had begun acting.

Opening the back door, he smiled when he heard the scream followed by the loud shotgun blast, thinking to himself, 'So much for that bitch!'

Chapter 2

Pooh looked at the phone with a confused look on his face, as it was the fifth time the unknown number had called his phone. Had he not been lying next to his main bitch, Bailey, he would have answered it, snapping on whoever the fuck was blowing his phone up. Everybody already knew that was a no-go!

Shit, if he didn't answer, he just didn't answer, meaning he was busy, in the middle of some shit, or more than likely spending quality time with his family. The way he was living, he spent as much time as possible with them, knowing that one day, he might not make it home.

The only exception to that was for his big brother, Memphis, as not even his last breath could stop him from being there if his brother needed him.

Glancing to his left, he saw Bailey shaking her head while mumbling under her breath. Without a doubt, wrong or right, he knew an argument was coming. Anytime she suspected something or didn't get her way, her attitude went from 0 to 100 before he could find a way to get out of dodge.

Trying not to ruin the beautiful evening that they had been having, he looked her in the eyes and said, "Baby, I don't know who the *fucc* that is, steady blowing up my shit. But I'm here with you, so fucc them!"

His twin and mini-me, Lil' Pooh, barely three years old, looked at his mom, smiling, and said, "Yeah, Ma! The movie still on, so fuck them!"

Bailey got madder as both her son and baby's daddy cracked up, laughing together. *They're probably laughing at me,* she thought.

Throwing the remote control at the wall, she screamed, "Well, call them the fuck back and see who the fuck it is since it ain't no pressure!"

Before Pooh could respond and dig in her ass for acting like that in front of his son, his phone rang again with the same unfamiliar number.

Picking it up, he screamed, "Who the fuck is this!" He put it on speakerphone, not giving a fuck if it was one of his side bitches or not, especially after that lil' stunt Bailey just pulled in front of their son. Hell, she would be lucky if all he did was choke slam her lil' ass. She knew that it was zit zero arguing in front of their son.

He was just about to tell her just how the fuck he felt until he lost all train of thought, hearing the operator tell him he had a prepaid call from his brother's right-hand man, Bronze.

Accepting the free call, he walked out of ear range while wondering what could be so important for his brother's friend to be banging his line like that, especially considering the fact that he didn't fuck with him like that.

Plus, there was still unfinished beef between them after he had not only fucked and dogged Bronze's baby mama out, but he had also broadcasted it for all the jokes and bullshit Bronze had pulled on him growing up.

Chapter 3

Toya had stopped to fill up her tank and grab a few things for her 6 a.m. to 2 p.m. shift at the punk ass county jail. For the hundredth time, she shook her head, laughing, thinking about how out of all the things she despised in the world, the police were number one, yet there she was, a fucking detention officer.

That was something she never would've even considered until her son-in-law, Memphis, tricked her by giving her $5,000 to just get the job and then another $5,000 after she was hired to sneak his homeboy a phone and something to blow on while fighting his murder charge.

Yeah, they both knew he could've gotten it done for a fraction of the cost or maybe even for free by fucking with one of the many CO bitches that were always DM'n him and on his dick, but he didn't want to jeopardize his homie even more by having the bitch flip when he cut the bitch off after she was done.

Plus, he didn't trust bitches to be all up in his business. Not only did they act purely off emotions, but they also knew how to both lie their asses off and manipulate their way into the front and back end of the operation, possibly taking control of it by running to another nigga with the scheme the first time they didn't get their way.

With the type of money that could be made, he didn't want to take that chance. He knew there was stupid money to be made by flooding the jail with whatever was wanted or needed in that bitch.

Toya couldn't agree more. Hell, since starting, she had bought herself a brand-new truck, paid off all her student loans, paid up all her bills, and had stacked up a nice lil' goose egg for a rainy day and a nice ass vacation, all thanks to him.

Plus, she had always dreamed about going on a cruise, which was what she was thinking about when her daughter, Queen, called her to let her know that Memphis had left something and some money at the house for her that he wanted her to get before she went to work.

Wanting to see her daughter but get the money even more, Toya was jumping into her truck when she saw Memphis's brother, Strip, across the street, living up to his name by making two niggas strip. For the life of her, she couldn't understand how niggas could be so tough one minute and so pussy the next. Like, to her, a man had to be pussy to allow another man to make him strip like a bitch on a pole until she looked back over and saw the big ass stick Strip was pointing at both now-naked men.

Being herself, she couldn't help laughing when she thought about how cold it was outside and the fact that both now-naked men had to be freezing their asses off. Then she started laughing harder, on the brink of tears, when she pictured both niggas shaking like bitches in a club. Rumor had it that Strip wasn't shit to be played with.

She was wiping her eyes when she saw flashes across the street and realized that Strip had then shot both people. Going off instinct, she threw the truck into drive and floored it across the street. Jumping the curb, she screamed for Strip to come on as he calmly stood over both now-dead bodies, continuing to load the bodies with shot after shot until she heard a click.

"What the fuck were you thinking!" she screamed at Strip while trying to get them as far away from the murder scene as possible.

"Sending a fuckin' message," Strip calmly replied in his deep voice. "Now, slow this motherfucka down before you get us pulled over," he said, staring at her. Hearing her suck her teeth, he wondered if he should kill her ass, too, for seeing what she had just seen. Yeah, she may've been Memphis's wife's mother, but she wasn't shit to him. Plus, he didn't trust anybody with a badge, no matter what kind it was.

Toya was shaking her head, still fuming, not aware of how close to death she was. So she snapped, saying, "You niggas so stupid! Y'all just run around shooting and killing niggas, not caring who may be around or watching."

Gritting his teeth, Strip yelled, "Shut the fuck up, as you should be thanking me," while staring her upside her head.

She shook her head, thinking, *the nerve of this nigga.* "Thanking you for what?" she screamed. "When I just saved you and helped you get away from a fuckin' murder scene!"

Snarling, he barked, "First, how about you watch yo' smart ass mouth and forget what the fuck you just saw. Second, like I said, thanking me for saving yo' ass from being the victim at the would've-been robbery/homicide them two clown, snitching ass niggas was about to commit, had I not killed them!" Continuing, he said, "I mean, open yo' fuckin' eyes and think about the odds of them two niggas and me being there across the street from you at 5:20 a.m., especially when you think about the fact that I don't even get out of bed before one o'clock in the fuckin' afternoon. Plus, yo' daughter already called you, right? Right?"

"Yeah," Toya stammered, answering while wondering what the fuck was going on.

Smirking, he knew he pissed her off even more when he barked, "It ain't no package for you to take to work today. I'm the fuckin' package! The money there waiting for you is yours for safely getting me to my brother's house."

Toya was confused before once again being impressed by the way Memphis operated. Instead of exposing his hand by worrying people or asking others to do something, Memphis simply told the right people what to do, and sat back, watching it unfold, which was another reason he made her sick.

"Thank you," Toya sincerely told Strip. "Although I do have one question," she said. "Why did you make them strip if you knew you were gonna kill them anyway?"

Smirking while staring at the attractive, slightly older woman, Strip said, "Like I first told you, to send a message that our family is not to be fucked with. Now, shut up and drive."

What Strip didn't say was that he hadn't gotten his hands dirty in a minute and had to live up to his name's sake, letting the rest of the jack boys and up-and-coming wolves know that he was still very much active in the streets.

Chapter 4

Chauncey ran into his first major problem after first stepping out of the door. It wasn't the knee-high snow or the below-freezing weather. Being born and raised in Fargo, ND, he was used to all those elements. It was the fact that he didn't have his keys, and being on a Rez in North Dakota with no wheels, in the absolute middle of nowhere, was like him in the middle of a women's prison yard with nothing on, dick just swinging, especially when he heard shouts and shots coming from behind him.

Not to mention, daylight was quickly approaching, and being a nigga running around with nothing on but boxers, shoes, and a bulletproof vest, the Rez was the quickest way in life to either go to jail or hell. He didn't know which would be worse—being spotted again by the natives, who were for sure still looking for him, or the federates, who would take him to the middle of the desert and kill his black ass out there, leaving his body to be devoured by coyotes or some shit.

He ran into his second biggest problem, coming around a bend, startling a wild pack of Rez dogs that, at times, could be just as vicious as starving pit bulls or wolves, especially during the winter, when food was scarce as hell on the ground. Instead of slowing down or turning around, without hesitation, he aimed at the biggest one, letting off a couple of shots as he noticed a car turning into a gas station a couple of blocks ahead.

He was hoping that if he was fast enough and could catch up to whoever was behind the wheel, he might have just had a chance out of this fucked up, sticky situation.

Turning up the speed, he gave it all he had. He was looking up, thinking he had just about made it, when he felt the first bite to the back of his leg. Ignoring the pain, refusing to give up, he thought he saw daylight until the second bite to his other leg tripped him up, causing him to not only bust his ass going down but also feel like he broke his wrist when trying to stop the fall.

"No!" he screamed. *I can't die like some white, blonde bitch in a horror scene,* he thought.

Rolling over, he let off shot after shot until the slide on the gun stayed open. Realizing he was out of bullets and possibly time, he stood up and limped as quickly as he could toward the gas station parking lot, leaving a trail of blood behind him.

Chapter 5

"You may begin speaking now."

"Hello? Hello?" Bronze urgently said, glad to finally get an answer.

"This shit better be good," Pooh said, still wondering why the fuck Bronze had been blowing up his phone.

"Aye, lil' nigga, you can kill all that tough-guy shit. I ain't even call for all that," Bronze stated, trying to keep his composure.

"Why the fuck you been banging my line like a bitch for?" Pooh asked, seeing that he was getting under Bronze's skin.

Bronze laughed, still picturing the lil' boy that always followed him and his best friend, Memphis, around. Deep down inside, he loved the lil' nigga like his own brother and knew that he could never truly hurt him. Hell, the kid didn't even realize it, but he had pushed him as much as he could or that Memphis would allow, making him into the beast he was today.

Shaking his head, he took a deep breath and said, "I'ma beat yo' ass like I used to when I come home. In the meantime, them people just left, asking me questions about you, Strip, and Blacc. Plus, Folks upstairs sent a message down to me that Two Feet been leaving the pod for hours at a time with no real valid explanation. Plus, they overheard the nigga on the phone, telling his bitch that he would be home soon, which don't even sound right with everything he facing, unless it's something I don't know. Shit, you know better than anybody that your brother can turn wheels that

14

supposedly can't be turnt, which is why I ain't gave lil' Folks upstairs the green light to X dat nigga out yet," Bronze said.

"Damn," Pooh said, calming down for the first time since answering the phone. "Have you talked to my brother or anybody else yet?" Pooh asked.

"Nawl! Me and your brother got a specific time we talk, and I didn't wanna wait. Dat nigga Strip phone been going straight to voicemail, and for some reason, the nigga Blacc phone off. Now thinking about it, when was the last time you seen or talked to dat nigga?" Bronze asked.

"Shit, me and bro was just asking each other the same shit a few days ago, and neither one of us had an answer," Pooh stated, starting to get paranoid. "Now that I'm thinking about it, what the fuck you say to them people, and why the fuck you ain't use the baby (cell phone) to call me?" Pooh asked.

"First off, lil' bro or not, I'll bury yo' ass and be at yo' funeral if you ever say or imply what the fuck you just did to me again. Second, when I got back to my cell, I could tell someone had been in there, and when I checked on the baby, I could tell she wasn't sleeping like I had left her, so I flushed that bitch," Bronze heatedly replied.

Pooh, realizing who he was talking to, mentally kicked himself in the ass. Bronze was one of the four people in the world that he never had to worry about snitching, and that was something he was willing to stake his life on.

Plus, although he would never verbally apologize to Bronze, or any man for that matter, he did feel slightly bad, as he knew without a shadow of a doubt that Bronze would never cross his brother.

"Damn, Bronze," Pooh said, "I hate to cut you off, my nigga, but I need to holla at my brother asap. All this shit ain't sitting right with me."

"Yeah, me either," Bronze said.

"In the meantime, you straight in there, big homie, or need anything?" Pooh asked.

Bronze busted out laughing and said, "Let me find out."

"Fuck you laughing at?" Pooh asked while laughing.

"A flashback," Bronze stated. "But shit, lil' nigga, just do me a favor by you and Strip getting low until big bro can figure all this shit out."

"That's a bet," Pooh said, still laughing before hanging up.

Chapter 6

Toya was deep in thought as she got off the exit a few minutes away from her daughter and Memphis's house. As bad as she wanted to ask Strip why someone wanted to rob, let alone kill her, she didn't, because something in her told her to leave the killer alone, as he had asked.

Plus, she honestly didn't want to look a gift horse in its mouth, as her mom used to say. She was just glad to be alive, thinking about what could have happened.

She was turning into her daughter's neighborhood when Strip suddenly sat up and told her to stop. Although slightly confused, she knew better than to question him, especially after what she had just seen. She was even more confused when Strip told her to call her fucking daughter and place it on speaker.

Holding her tongue, she did what he asked, but she made a mental note to herself to check his ass before he got out of her truck for talking to her like that. She was even laughing to herself, thinking about all she was going to say when her daughter's voicemail picked up. Looking at the phone confusedly, she immediately called back, knowing she had just talked to Queen, only to get the voicemail again.

Looking at Strip as to say, "What now?" she noticed that his attention was focused on the cars up the street.

Knowing something wasn't right, Strip placed a fresh magazine in the AR-15 and was opening the door, about to tell Toya to circle the block, when her phone rang. Seeing her sort of relax, he figured it was Queen and nodded, telling her to place it on speaker.

He instantly knew something was wrong by the way Queen came on excitedly. Knowing the relationship Toya and Queen had, he knew it was fake. They always argued over Memphis. Toya felt like her daughter was too good for Memphis, yet Queen loved him more than she did God and was too happy to tell the world about it.

Even Toya was confused, as Queen acted like they hadn't talked in days, even going as far as asking her how her ex-husband, Bubba, was doing, when they had been separated for years.

Toya was playing along until Queen interrupted her by saying that she had to go, but not to forget to hide the package she had picked up for Bubba. Toya was laughing, saying she would, when she noticed that Queen had already hung up.

Chapter 7

Stacy was lost, pissed off, and confused as fuck. She had been driving around for the past hour with no reception, sense of direction, or real idea of where the fuck she was.

All she knew was she was on what they called the Rex, which, in actuality, was just a big ass, old country town in the middle of no fucking where that the government had placed a lot of natives, which was what she thought to herself anyway.

The truth of the matter was that she was mad at her dumb ass big brother, Memphis, who could have sent anybody in the fucking world out there, but he had chosen her. Granted, he would have never sent her or given her anything illegal to do, had she not lied and stolen his big-body Benz.

Hell, he probably would have forgiven her for both, had her drinking not gotten her into an accident, which led to the discovery of his stash spot that was not empty. It had cost him not only his car and whatever was in it, but also almost a quarter million dollars that he somehow came up with to have the charges and case swept under the rug.

Shit, she was so grateful not to go to jail that she promised him she would do anything, with no questions asked, to help repay him for everything that she had cost him, which, in turn, led her to the middle of nowhere in North Dakota.

She was still fuming when she saw a gas station up ahead. Rolling in, she thought her luck had changed when she saw a payphone, something she didn't think existed anymore outside of airports. She was even more excited when not only did the phone work, but it was also answered on the second ring by Xavier, the person she was supposed to be meeting.

Xavier laughed at her misfortune of getting lost and said someone would be there in less than ten minutes. Not just wanting to sit around, she pulled up to the gas pump, figuring that she might as well fill up, use the restroom, and grab a few snacks for the return trip.

She was placing the nozzle back in the gas pump when she noticed an old ass F-150 pull into the lot and let a tall, lanky dude out. Ignoring them, she was turning to put the gas cap back on when her head was snatched back and repeatedly rammed on the roof of the car.

She thought she was being saved when the tall, lanky dude ran up, screaming, "Xavier said not to kill her until we get the work!" before jumping back in the F-150. She was losing consciousness when she saw a slim, black dude come into view and thought she heard a gunshot before everything went black.

Chapter 8

Pooh was thinking the worst while packing a small travel bag. He had attempted to contact both of his brothers over a dozen times with no answers, even going as far as to text them, something they never did, as his brother Memphis had taught him how the alphabet boys could retrieve text messages out of a phone, no matter how old they were or how you went about erasing them. If they got their hands on the phone, they could perform miracles with that bitch to place a nigga under the jail, which was why Memphis made it mandatory for everybody in their circle to get new phones every thirty to sixty days.

He was thinking about calling Queen, his brother's wife, but he didn't want to throw Memphis in a jam if he was just ducked off with a bitch or something, as they had both used each other as alibis several times to get away for a few hours.

At the same time, if anybody knew where Memphis was or what the fuck was going on, it would be Queen. She was also like that nigga's brain or second set of eyes or some shit, sometimes going as far as telling that nigga what he was thinking. Plus, like Bailey, not only didn't she play when it came to her man, but she also had a sharp ass tongue with an attitude that could go from 0 to 100 without any warning. That was why she and Bailey could never get along. Not to mention, Bailey was white, and Queen couldn't stand pink meat, male or female.

He was just about done packing his bag when Bailey busted into the room, throwing her phone at him. Dodging the phone, he was caught off guard by the two-piece she quickly followed up with. He was turning around to beat her ass for the old and the new, when he noticed that she had then grabbed one of the guns he had on the bed.

"Why, Pooh? Why!" she screamed with tears running from her eyes.

Pooh stood there, stuck, not knowing how to answer. Not only did it break his heart, seeing the pain written across her face, but he also didn't know which one of his dark secrets had come to the light. He knew whatever it was, it had to be big and deep, as he had never seen her this distraught.

He was about to open his mouth to speak when her next words froze him in place.

"How old is the baby?" she asked.

Once again caught off guard, Pooh just stood there, looking stupid.

"How old is the fuckin' baby!" she screamed while cocking the gun, aiming it at his head.

Chapter 9

Toya was as confused as ever. After turning around and throwing her phone out the window like Strip had told her to do, she aimlessly drove north, making random turns to see if Strip would say something. Each time, she became even more pissed off, confused, and distraught when he didn't.

She was beginning to think he was as lost as she was, or asleep, when suddenly, he told her to make the next right. Quickly turning with hopes of a destination in mind, she was once again confused when he asked her to pull over up ahead before fully going over the bridge they were riding across.

Watching him hop out of the truck, she began to understand what he was up to when she saw him wiping the AR-15 off before lobbing it off the bridge. Even his next words made sense when he told her they needed to get a new phone before getting off the road.

Thinking quickly, she remembered she still had two new phones that Memphis had given her to pass on in the back seat, but she hadn't had a chance to do so yet. She was reaching behind her seat to grab one of them when she saw the blue lights in her rearview mirror.

Chapter 10

Chauncey was opening his third energy drink when he saw the radio flash with another incoming phone call. For some reason, someone named Queen had been steadily blowing the lil' sexy, red-bone chick lying in the back seat up repeatedly.

He was about to ignore it again when the car beside him suddenly swerved into his lane, cutting him off, causing him to not only slam on the brakes but also to hit the accept button instead of the ignore.

Cursing under his breath, he was about to hang the call up until a worried voice seemed to come from everywhere at once, saying, "Stacy? Stacy, girl, where you at? You been had me so worried about you!"

He was once again about to hang up by hitting the end button, simply thinking it was one of the girl homegirls or something, looking for her, until the next words gave him pause.

"Stacy, you better answer me and let me know you okay before your brother sends out a whole fuckin' hit squad to find you, and you know I'm not playin'."

He wondered who the girl or her brother was, as well as what she was even doing on the Rez, as he could tell she didn't belong there. He hesitantly answered, saying, "I don't know who this is, but the girl that was driving this car had an accident and is passed out in the back seat."

Instead of relief or gratitude, like he thought was coming, he was surprised when the voice went from worried to

SAVAGE DREAMZ | KING DAVID

authoritative, saying, "Who the fuck is this, and what type of accident got her passed out in the back seat?"

He was deciding on how much to say over the phone when he was interrupted by the voice saying, "Fuck that! Is she okay, and where the fuck are y'all?"

Sensing this was not someone to be ignored, he answered, saying, "Yeah, she breathing, but she done lost a lot of blood."

Queen immediately responded with, "Where the fuck are y'all, and why didn't you take her to the hospital or emergency room?"

Chauncey answered, saying, "I can't say why over this phone or do that in my current predicament, as I need medical attention too. But we're on Hwy I-295, going south toward South Dakota."

"Okay," Queen answered, slightly calming down. "Keep heading south, and I'm going to call you back in less than ten minutes to tell you where to go. But look. I don't know who you are, so all I'ma say is this. If that girl dies, her brothers will never stop hunting you and everyone else that was involved," she said before hanging up.

Shaking his head while pounding the steering wheel, Chauncey wondered what the fuck he had gotten himself into.

Chapter 11

Pooh, seeing that his silence wasn't helping the situation, opted for the truth by saying, "Bae, on some real shit, I don't know what the fuck you talking about. Our son is the only child I got."

Bailey, not believing a word his lying ass was saying, moved the gun down to his chest so she couldn't miss him, saying, "Oh, yeah. So some random bitch name Annie just called, playing on my phone, talking about 'tell Pooh his new baby need diapers' just to fuck with me, huh?"

"Annie?" he questioned. "I don't even know no fuckin' Annie!" Pooh yelled, getting pissed off at the whole situation. Had it been one of the hoes he had been recently fucking, he may have claimed up, trying to buy some time to get the gun out of her hands. But having her name a bitch he knew for a fact he hadn't fucked caused his blood pressure to boil. He was tired of random hoes playing games, trying to break up his happy home.

"Yeah, bitch, Annie!" Bailey screamed. "The same bitch that's taking her family to see your first love!"

"What the fuck?" he yelled, shaking his head, trying to make sure he was hearing her correctly. "I don't know no fuckin' Annie!" he was screaming until everything clicked into place, and he couldn't help laughing out loud.

His brother, Memphis, had done it again. He was still holding his stomach, laughing, about to tell Bailey what was going on, when the gun went off, striking the wall, just inches above his head.

"What the fuck!" he screamed, rushing Bailey, not caring if she shot him or not. Reaching her, he snatched the gun out of her hands and was reaching back to slap fire out of her ass when Lil' Pooh came running into the room, having been woken up from his sleep.

"Dad! Mom!" Lil' Pooh cried, seeing the tension between them. Looking confused, the lil' boy didn't know who to reach for.

Pooh, taking the initiative, tucked the gun in his waistline while picking his son up. Turning to Bailey, he shook his head, saying, "It's a message from my fuckin' brother. Dummy! Annie is what we jokingly call Rose (Queen's sister) behind her back because she always acting like a old woman or someone's auntie. Her saying my new baby needs diapers is saying my new phone is tapped or dirty, and her saying she's taking her family to see my first love is saying they going to my grandmother, my first love, Ma Dear's house because shit is getting hot, so I need to send y'all too, which is why she directed it at you."

Bailey fell to the floor with a dumb ass look on her face. Everything Pooh said sounded genuine and made perfect sense. She even had to give it to Memphis for knowing to have a bitch call her phone, talking about Pooh, as she was gon' get the message to him no matter what she had to do to find his ass. She was still sitting on the floor when her phone started ringing again.

Chapter 12

Queen was sitting in the house, damn near pulling her loc's out. Not only did she not know where the fuck her husband was, but she knew for a fact that the feds and whoever else were sitting outside her house, possibly listening to every call that came in or out of their four-bedroom, three-bath baby mansion.

No, they weren't rich, by far, but they were happy and content with their home and lifestyle. Not to mention Memphis had promised her the world, and she knew he was a man of his word, so this was just the beginning.

She also knew that when Memphis wasn't home or available, she was the boss, and he expected her to perform her duties as he would, which was another reason she was sitting at the table, damn near losing her mind. It seemed like everything that could go wrong had, and that shit was still coming at her in every single direction.

On top of that, every time one of the dogs growled, she thought one of the doors was about to come crashing in.

Granted, she knew nothing illegal was in the house, as they both had learned the hard way what that brought or could lead to. Plus, after the last time, Memphis had promised never to place her in harm's way again, so she was content that if they did kick the door in, they wouldn't find anything.

What was bothering her the most was trying to find out not only where the fuck everybody was but also how to direct everyone, knowing her phone was tapped, and Memphis had strictly forbidden her from ever texting anyone in their circle anything that could one day come back to bite them in the ass.

She thought she had made a little leeway when she was able to warn Strip through her mother. She knew Strip was like Memphis and paranoid about everything, so he would've read between the lines. Plus, the lights on top of the house were a red flag, warning anyone in their circle that the house wasn't safe.

She even had slightly relaxed when her sister had stepped by to bring the dog food she did every other day, and she was able to convey a message through her to Pooh. She was just hoping that his dumb ass baby mama got the message correctly instead of getting all emotional and in her feelings like she always did. That was another reason she couldn't stand white people.

Then, in the blink of an eye, everything turned from sugar to shit. While trying to reach Stacy, her worst fears of a snake in their circle were confirmed when an unfamiliar number called her phone. Quickly answering it, hoping it was Memphis, she was completely surprised and caught off guard not only hearing DJ's voice but also him asking if he could come by the house to pick up his usual.

Acting totally confused, she told him that he had the wrong number and immediately hung up, just to see him call back three additional times.

Then things really turned from bad to worse when Stacy's phone was answered not by her but by some nigga saying that Stacy was hurt and couldn't be taken to an emergency room. By his tone and the way he spoke, she could tell he was in the streets. Thinking about it now, she was happy about that, as his street instinct kept him from saying anything incriminating over the phone.

Knowing Strip was the right person to put on that, she attempted to call her mom back several times, only to have it keep going unanswered. She was contemplating calling Butch, Stacy's father, but she knew Memphis would bust a blood vessel if she asked that nigga for anything or placed him in their business. Plus, the nigga was slow, she thought, and so she knew she would have to explain it to him several times before he caught on. Not to mention, she couldn't take the chance of him saying the wrong thing over the phone.

Shaking her head, knowing she had to move quickly, she picked up the phone and called the one person she couldn't stand the most.

Chapter 13

Strip was contemplating hopping out and making a run for it, when Toya handed him the new phone, telling him to relax. He was even more pissed off at himself for not following his first instinct when he saw that, instead of one officer, there were two of them, with one coming up on his side of the truck with his hand resting on his firearm.

Ignoring the officer on his side, he continued to activate the new phone while Toya prepared to hand her driver's license and registration to the officer on her side. Thinking about the two bodies that he had just left stanking, he jumped when the officer on his side knocked on the window and told him to roll it down. Looking at Toya with an evil glare, he vowed to himself that he was gon' kill her if they took him in—even just for questioning.

He was rolling down his window, thinking of a lie to tell, when the officer on Toya's side suddenly peered in the window, seeing the guards' uniform, and smiled when he noticed who was driving.

"Ms. Alston, what you doing, speeding?" he jokingly asked while telling his partner to relax.

Toya smiled, seeing the officer who was always bringing in drunken drivers and other offenders during the early hours of the morning. "Trying to get to work," she answered. Glancing at the time, she continued by saying, "I'm already late. My shift started about fifteen minutes ago."

Shining his flashlight around the inside of the truck, he stopped on Strip and looked at Toya, saying, "And who's this fellow?"

Toya smiled again, knowing that, on several occasions, the officer—she couldn't even remember his name—had tried to flirt with her. "My boyfriend. He's dropping me off so I don't have to try to find a parking spot and walk all the way to the front," she answered.

She had to refrain from laughing when she saw the embarrassed and disappointed look on the officer's face, and she couldn't help smirking when the officer told her he was letting her off with a warning before walking back to his police cruiser with his head down.

Pulling off, she started laughing until Strip tried snatching her head back, only for the wig she was wearing to end up in his hand. Looking at the wig, confused, he turned toward her and asked her what the fuck her problem was, only to get punched in the nose, totally catching him off guard.

"I'm sick of this shit!" she screamed while pulling over on a side street. "First, I watched you stand over two motherfuckas, giving them every shot you had. Second, you tell me them same two motherfuckas was about to rob and kill me for some ungodly reason. Then my fuckin' daughter called me, sounding scared, talking crazy as hell, with you being rude ass fuck to me. Now, you got a choice, motherfucka. You can get out of my truck right here and now, or you can tell me what the fuck you and your brothers got me and my babies involved in."

Strip was staring at Toya, debating on how much his brother would want her to know, when the burnt orange Trackhawk bent the corner they were parked on. Thinking quickly, Strip told Toya, "I'll tell you as much as I can, but first, I need you to please follow that fuckin' truck."

Chapter 14

Chauncey was entering South Dakota when he first began to feel lightheaded and exhausted. Fearing the worst, as his whole left side had gone completely numb, he began looking around for another energy drink or anything with sugar. He knew for a fact he couldn't take the chance of entering any store in his attire or condition.

He debated pulling over when the phone rang again. Looking at the time, he noticed that only eight minutes had passed. He debated answering or ignoring it when the phone stopped ringing and immediately began again. Remembering the words the chick said, he grudgingly answered, not knowing what to expect.

He was highly surprised by Queen's tone of voice when she said, "Hey, Tee. I don't know why the fuck you didn't answer the first couple times I called, but I wouldn't advise you doing that again. In the meantime, love, I found a vet for both puppies that's open 24/7 and accepts walk-ins. He's directly south of you in Des Moines, Iowa. If you got a pen, I'll happily give you the address."

Confused by her tone of voice but understanding exactly what she was saying, he responded with, "I'm driving, shorty. Text me the addy!"

He wasn't sure what happened, but he felt the ice in her voice when she said, "I ain't your shorty, bitch, and I hate repeating myself!"

He was tired of her shit talking and was about to give it to her ass and bang, when he suddenly heard a moan, followed by, "Damn, Queen, why you steady yelling?" from the back seat.

Chapter 15

Bailey was getting off the floor when Pooh tossed her the phone, saying, "It's my grandmother. Ignore that shit, and pack you and the baby a small bag." Bailey instead answered, knowing that if she ignored Ms. Rhonda, she was gon' simply call back-to-back 'til she got an answer, especially knowing that Lil' Pooh wasn't in daycare due to his daddy being so overprotective. Not to mention, his two uncles loved getting their nephew to spoil.

Taking a deep breath to calm herself, she said, "Hey, Ms. Rhonda. How you doing today?"

"I'm fine, baby," Ms. Rhonda answered. "Just sitting here with Whitney, wondering how our grandbaby doing."

Hearing them, Pooh set the baby on the bed, shaking his head, knowing his grandmother loved to talk. True indeed, he loved his grandmother almost as much as he loved his mother, but he also knew when she got an audience, she was gon' take full advantage and not to be forgotten or outdone. If his mother was anywhere close by, she, too, was gon' get her time as well.

It surprised him when he came out of the restroom from flushing his cellphone to see Bailey holding the baby with a small bag packed. "What the fuck?" he jokingly asked. "That must be a world record," he said while laughing.

"Not at all," Bailey said. "Now grab yo' bag and hurry up! We gotta drop the baby off at your mother's, grab you a new phone, and find out what the fuck going on."

"Hold on, hold on," Pooh said with a mug on his face. "What you mean, *we*?"

"Nigga, just what the fuck I said," Bailey answered with a matching mug. "I saw the bag you packed, so whatever the fuck you about to get into, I'ma be right beside you. Now hurry up and grab yo' bag, like I fuckin' said, because if Memphis say or think it might not be safe, then we need to get as far from here as fast as we can. I've never known him to send bullshit warnings."

Knowing she was right, Pooh rushed into the room, grabbing his bag and vest.

Chapter 16

Queen was rolling a blunt, thinking about taking another shot, wondering if she had made the right calls or not. Yes, she knew better than to second-guess herself; she just wasn't sure who all in their circle she could trust.

She had already made a mental note to herself to check the fuck out of Twist as soon as she laid eyes on her. Hell, she already couldn't stand the bitch. She felt like Twist was a snake in the making, willing to sell her loyalty to the highest bidder. But the bitch had royally fucked up this time by questioning her rank or authority, especially over an open line.

If it weren't for the fact that Stacy was in dire need of medical attention in the middle of no-fuckin'-where, she would've sent one of the guys to have the bitch brought to her so she could beat the hoe on sight. The shit was personal now and long overdue between them.

Second, she had called Tone, Memphis's dad, who was their go-to guy on stash spots and anything else dealing with any of the cars. Knowing that once any one of Stacy's brothers, especially Strip, found out what had taken place with their baby sister, all hell was gon' break out over North Dakota. She knew she had to have a truck or SUV already filled with as much artillery as it could hold and already on the road there. There wasn't shit that was gon' stop one, if not all, of the brothers from killing everyone involved.

Third, before calling Stacy back, she called Slim and Dee, two of their hitters, telling them they were added to the roster in Des Moines, Iowa, of all places, knowing her big daddy would want loyal protection around Stacy as soon as possible.

She grew frustrated, calling Stacy's phone until it was finally answered. Knowing that others were listening, she masked her feelings and voice, trying her hardest not to blow up on whoever the fuck was answering and driving Stacy's car, but she lost it when the fuck nigga came slick out of his mouth.

She, however, was relieved, hearing Stacy's voice until Stacy told her that the guy who saved her life was bleeding bad and barely conscious.

Hating that Stacy was panicking and saying too much over the phone, she quickly calmed her down and gave her the address to the vet, slyly letting her know that professional dog handlers were on the way to help.

Finally, she called Slim's wife, Key, telling her to pull up. Even though Key wasn't street, she was loyal and could be trusted. Plus, she was smart enough not to ask any questions. She knew if Queen was calling her, telling her to pull up, it had to be serious.

She debated whether to call Blacc again. It was strange how the nigga hadn't called or been seen, with everything going on. She had even tried calling Mandy, Blacc's baby mama, only to find out it had been disconnected. Smoking her blunt, she wondered for the hundredth time what was going on and where the fuck her husband was.

Chapter 17

Strip couldn't believe his eyes and would've killed anybody trying to tell or convince him of what he was witnessing. Following the burnt-orange Trackhawk that he, himself, had bought for his childhood friend, Wiz, when he first came home from prison, turned out to be painful as fuck.

Wiz was supposed to be locked up, preparing for trial for the two bodies he had caught outside Waffle House, when a Barney Rubble-looking motherfucka tried to intervene and stop Wiz from leaving the scene after Wiz had smoked the nigga trying to rob him for the half of a brick he was there to sell him.

If that wasn't bad enough, seeing DJ hop out of the passenger side was even more confusing because the nigga Wiz had popped was DJ's cousin; and knowing DJ the way he did, he knew DJ wouldn't just let that go or ride that easy, even if just to save face in the streets. DJ was somewhat an up-and-coming rapper in the city, and although half the shit he rapped about was all cap, the other half he rapped about was dead on.

The nigga DJ really did have more than a few bodies under his belt and was quick to up the pole when tried or disrespected. His biggest problem, though, was hustling. For some reason, the nigga was always fuckin' up the bag or pack, to the point that Memphis stopped giving the nigga work and simply put him on with his hitters.

That was cool at first, until the lil' nigga started rapping about the missions they were hitting or going on in his rap songs. To keep the circle safe, Memphis even cut him out of that, opting instead to put the money he was paying him behind the nigga's rap career, only for the nigga to miss show after show he'd been able to get booked for him.

Memphis wasn't losing any sleep over it until it started making Queen's promotion company look bad with different venues. No one wanted to work with a company they couldn't depend on.

But the killer and what really broke Strip's heart was when the smoke-gray Dodge Charger pulled up, and the two detectives got out, quickly approaching DJ and Wiz, shaking their hands. He even let a tear fall from his eye when he saw Wiz hand over what looked like a small tape.

Chapter 18

Stacy was pacing the small clinic, not knowing what to do or think. After wrestling to get the guy out of the driver's seat and into the back, she had driven like she was in a high-speed chase, only stopping once to fill up. She didn't even take the time to go in or use the restroom, considering the fact that she was covered in his blood and hers.

Her brother would just have to understand, as he strictly forbade using any type of credit or bank cards while taking care of business. She just couldn't take the chance of someone asking questions. Plus, she had attempted to call her brother several times, each call going straight to voicemail. She even tried to call Queen back, but it went unanswered, which caused her to panic even more, as one of them was always available.

Hell, she was still surprised that they had even made it. She still didn't even know who the guy was or what all had taken place to get them there. All she remembered before blacking out was hearing a gunshot.

After getting stitched up and being attended to, she was approached by the head doctor, who told her that the guy she had brought in with her had sustained multiple injuries, including a gunshot to the left thigh and kidney area, the last being stopped by the bulletproof vest he wore. Though it stopped the bullet, it had bruised several ribs that would hurt like hell. He also told her they had stitched up several wounds in his legs that appeared to be caused by canines of some sort.

The doctor was attempting to ask her about his patient's last tetanus shot when they heard a scream, followed by several loud voices coming from the room where the dude had been taken to. Running in, they noticed one doctor lying on the floor, not moving, with several nurses trying desperately to get the dude to put down the scalpel he was swinging.

Stacy, seeing the type of reaction before, couldn't help but double over in laughter, causing everyone in the room to turn toward her.

Chauncey, seeing the pretty red bone's face, slightly relaxed and was attempting to stand up straight when he felt the worst pain he'd ever felt and blacked out. Several hours had passed before he woke up again. Beginning to panic, he was about to rip the IV out of his arm when he felt a hand telling him it was okay and to relax.

Not wanting to admit to the pretty girl that he was afraid of hospitals, he instead asked her where his pole was. She had just handed him the gun when two niggas he had never seen entered his room with murderous scowls on their faces.

Chapter 19

Pooh was shaking his head, laughing, watching Bailey come out of his mother's house after dropping Lil' Pooh off. He couldn't believe she had fallen for the okey doke again. Watching Bailey open the passenger door, he was already reciting the words she was about to say. There was no way possible his mother was about to let anyone, especially one of her kids, get away without taking her to the store first. True indeed, she had several of her own vehicles that they had bought or just given her over the years, but to her, having a chance of interrogating someone, especially one of her kids, was priceless.

"Ms. Whitney needs a quick ride to the store," Bailey mumbled.

"What?" Pooh asked, getting the full enjoyment of it.

"Yo' mama need a fuckin' ride to the store," Bailey repeated.

Pooh, not liking her attitude, decided to fuck with her more. "Why didn't you tell her no?" he responded. "You know we in a rush."

Bailey's whole face turned bright red in embarrassment, and she answered in that sweet, innocent voice he had fallen in love with. "You know I can't tell yo' mama no. It's rude, and she'll never forgive me."

Pooh laughed, knowing that his mother knew how Bailey felt and took full advantage of the opportunity each time. True enough, she loved Bailey and even came to like and respect her for standing next to her baby boy after all these years. Still, with his mom being from the south, she didn't trust white people at all and felt like they all had hidden agendas, no matter who they were or how hard they smiled in your face.

Pooh was getting out to move the bag of guns out of sight when the lime-green Dodge Challenger bent the corner. Being in Avondale, AZ, it was common to see all types of new and old muscle cars, as rich white people loved their toys.

What gave Pooh pause and allowed his street instinct to kick in was hearing loud drill music and seeing the out-of-state tag on the front of the car. He was still about to ignore his instincts, knowing that only a handful of people knew where his mother stayed, until he saw what appeared to be a stick get passed to the passenger from the back seat of the car.

Chapter 20

Queen was sitting in her game chair in their game room, playing *Call of Duty: Black Ops 6*, when she noticed one of their Cane Corsos suddenly jump up, running toward the back of the house. Looking at the security monitor built in on the side of the TV, she saw a man in a mask and a bulletproof vest slide over the wall. Laughing, thinking she was finally about to use the new double-barreled pump-action shotgun she got for Christmas, she jumped up to run to Rosie's room, where they had to keep it since both she and Memphis were felons. She noticed another intruder slip over the wall.

As soon as the second intruder's feet touched the ground, two more of the dogs were off to investigate, knowing not to bark to alert whatever. That left Diamond, Queen's personal security dog, whining as if she, too, wanted a lil' adventure. Suddenly remembering the feds and whoever else was parked out front, she sighed too while patting Diamond's head. "I know, girl, I know. I wanna fuck them up too." She just knew the shotgun would be way too loud, and even though she knew she could justify it, she didn't have time or the patience to be answering any questions.

Sneaking to the back, she quietly opened the back door, letting the three growling dogs outside before running back to the game room to watch the action unfold. She had just sat back down when the phone rang, catching her off guard. Answering it without looking down, she was glad to hear it was a prepaid call from Bronze, knowing besides the boys,

Bronze would be next in line to know what the fuck was going on.

"Hello?" she said.

"Oh shit. Wassup, sis?"

"Shit, sitting in the game room, watching TV."

"Oh shit," Bronze said, laughing. "What you watching? One of those lil' investigation cop show shits y'all chicks seem to favor?" he asked, still laughing.

Laughing, she said, "Hell nawl! I got enough of that shit sitting right outside my front door. I'm watching two uninvited motherfuckas meet three viscous maneaters that probably weigh more than them!"

Bronze was quiet before saying, "Oh shit. In real life, sis?"

Nodding, she said, "Yeah, in real fuckin' life, bro!"

"Damn!" Bronze yelled. "I know bro can't be there then?" he asked

"Nawl, not right now," she answered, not wanting to indulge too much before she heard what he had to say. Instead, she asked, "What? You need me to stretch yo' books real quick?"

"Nawl! I need you to open yo' ears for a quick second," he said.

"Go ahead," she said. "But you know the way shit be these days. Motherfuckas always nosey!"

Laughing, he said, "I peep, so check it. I hit up baby boy this morning, letting him know Two-Feet in this bitch dancing to every song come on the radio! Like, that nigga even doing the "Remble" to oldies!"

"What the fuck?" she said while thinking about all the shit Two-Feet knew.

"Yeah, sis! On top of that, some OT niggas just got in here, saying they know and fuck with DJ and Wiz!"

"Wiz, Wiz?" she asked, confused.

"Yeah, sis! Wiz, Wiz! If that ain't enough *LifeTime* shit for yo' ass, I just heard it direct that Blacc don't play for the

45

team no more! He got drafted by a new team trying to come into the league!"

"Fuck no! It ain't no way, bro!" she said while watching one of the dogs bite down on one of the intruders' necks.

"I put that on 'B.O.S.', sis," Bronze said, knowing that all questioning about the matter would cease. "Word around the inside, he been trimming hedges around Mesa now."

"Fuck," she swore. As if she didn't have enough on her plate.

"I did hear from my lawyer, tho'. Two of the lying muffaccas that's trying to hang me were found ate up this morning."

"That's a bet," she said. "Motherfuckas should know by now they can't shit where they sleep!"

"Oh shit, I almost forgot, sis! I didn't get to work out this morning because they kept us locked down extra long. One of the guards told me they were supposedly waiting for some new guard or lady that works here or some shit!"

Queen shook her head, catching what was said while trying not to throw up from watching a couple of the dogs literally play tug of war with the last intruder's arm. "Listen, bro, I hate to cut this shit short, but the dogs just made a mess that I gotta clean up. In the meantime, jail ain't no place for dancing. Niggas too old for that shit," Queen said.

"Yeah?" Bronze asked.

"Hell yeah," Queen said with a smirk on her face, watching Key pull into her driveway.

Chapter 21

Strip was squeezing the phone so hard that Toya thought it would snap any second now. He had been constantly trying to reach both of his brothers repeatedly, with each of their phones going straight to voicemail. He had even attempted to call Queen back, but she didn't even answer. Everything in his gut told him the two snake motherfuckas across the street were either responsible or heavily involved in the mystery surrounding every fuckin' thing.

Toya just sat quietly, not knowing what to say to Strip, as she could literally see the steam coming off of him. "Fuck it. I'm in this far. What you wanna do?" she boldly asked.

"Shit, if I still had the AR, I'll hit all their snake asses," Strip said while gritting his teeth.

Toya thought deeply and quickly made a decision as she realized one, if not both, of her daughters were involved in whatever the fuck was going on. She said, "Look, I ain't got no AR, but I do have a thirteen if that would help."

"Huh?" Strip asked, puzzled by Toya's remark.

Toya reached on the side of her seat, coming out with a chrome Taurus 9mm.

"What the fuck?" Strip asked. "What would have happened if them crackers had asked us to step out of the truck, searched, and found that motherfucka?"

"Shit, I would've showed them my license permit to carry," she responded with a smile lighting up the truck.

"Damn, ma, I can't use that bitch if it's registered to you. The heat just gon' come back on us!"

"No, nigga! Just because I'm licensed don't mean I'm stupid. I'm from Cleveland, where shit go down every day. My registered one at home! This is its twin, my throwaway in case a motherfucka ever got too stupid with me."

Strip just shook his head, more curious about Toya than ever now. "My brother told me you was gangsta, but he didn't tell me you was rolling like this!" Strip replied.

"Well, it's a lot of things yo' brother and my babies don't know about me, and I'd appreciate it if it stayed that way. Now, again, what you wanna do, or better yet, how you wanna do this?" Toya asked, looking around.

"Well, it's daylight, and I don't want nobody seeing your truck or getting a chance to peep yo' tag number. Plus, I know for a fact that the two detectives are strapped. I just don't know about them other two rat motherfuckas," Strip said.

"So why not just wait until the two detectives leave?" Toya asked, clearly not liking what Strip was thinking.

"Because I gotta have that tape!" Strip said. "It ain't no telling what's all on that, and it could be the downfall of our family. So the gain definitely outweighs the risk."

Toya shook her head, knowing what Strip had just said could possibly be true. Although she didn't know everything they were into, she definitely had heard enough stories and rumors to know it was deep.

Strip was looking around when he suddenly looked at Toya, smiled, and said, "This is what I want you to do…"

Chapter 22

Chauncey's aim was dead on as he hid his pain, stepping in front of Stacy. "Put them shits down, and get the fuck out of here!" he barked, mugging both Slim and Dee.

For Slim and Dee's part, they simply smirked at the youngster, knowing that either one of them could've murked the youngster well before he upped or got out of the hospital bed. They both simply upped on sight, seeing Stacy with a stranger with a gun in hand. Either one of them would've died trying to save her instead of facing either of her brothers if she got hurt or injured in their presence. They had seen each one of them do some horrible, unimaginable shit, and they refused to fall victim to them.

"Nawl, youngster! You got the game fucked up! We ain't putting down shit until she's over here with us!" Dee said, inching closer.

Stacy suddenly came out of her trance of seeing the hurt and injured guy jumping up to protect her when he barely even knew her. She was trying to step from behind him when he gently pushed her back, saying, "Nawl, ma. I'll die before I let either of them take or hurt you!"

Blushing, Stacy said, "It's okay. I know them. They work for my brother!" Then she told Slim and Dee to put their guns down.

Neither Dee nor Slim wanted to put their guns down, not knowing the stranger, but after seeing his actions as well as hearing his words, they both knew that the youngster meant Stacy no harm. After they lowered their guns, Slim stepped forward. "Come on, Stacy. We got to get y'all the fuck out of here. It ain't no telling who know we all here or could possibly be on the way."

Stacy, knowing they could only be there on behalf of her brother, turned to her savior. "Trust me. It's okay. We need to listen to them. If they say we need to get out of here, we need to do it, and now."

Chauncey didn't know them or her brother and didn't trust anybody at the moment, but he heard the confidence and urgency in her voice and knew, in his current condition, he was better off with them than alone, especially since he didn't even know where the fuck he was. Lowering the gun, he tried to hide the pain but couldn't, causing him to lean over, grimacing in pain.

Laughing, Dee stepped forward. "Now that the masquerade's over, throw on yo' clothes, tough guy, so we can all get the fuck out of here!"

Stacy blushed again in embarrassment. "He ain't got no clothes!"

Dee and Slim looked at each other confusedly before asking, "Well, what the fuck did he come in here in?"

Stacy stepped over to the banister, picking up the bulletproof vest, turned to them and said, "Only this. They had to cut his boxers off."

Dee and Slim again looked at each other, both wondering the same thing. Who the fuck was this youngster, and what the fuck was he into?

Chapter 23

Pooh immediately went into beast mode, not caring if what he saw was accurate or not. Coming off his hip with the blick, he let the switch sing out before noticing Bailey had appeared beside him with an FN, gripping it with both hands just like he had taught her. It was crazy how he had started with eighty shots, while she only had fifty, yet he ran out of ammo way before she did.

He was reaching in the back for another clip and gun when he saw his mother appear on the front step of her house. He was screaming for her to go back into the house when he heard the car crash into something. Turning to see what had occurred, he saw the car had hit a brick-built mailbox. He was smiling to himself when he heard Bailey scream.

Seeing her crying and distraught, he rushed to her side, looking to see where she was hit, when she suddenly pointed behind him. Looking back, he saw his mother sprawled out on the steps of her porch with her head lying on the bottom step. Dropping his gun, he ran toward her, dropping to his knees when he reached her.

Seeing a bullet wound in her chest, he immediately thought the worst until he saw the slight rise and fall of her chest. He was taking his shirt off to press into the wound when he heard multiple shots come from behind him. Looking back, he saw Bailey standing over someone who had apparently climbed out of the car, shooting both his gun and hers at the dude while screaming.

It can't get any worse, he thought, until Lil' Pooh opened the door with his thumb in his mouth and asked him what was wrong with Nana. With tears in his eyes, Pooh yelled for Bailey, telling her to get the baby back in the house. His heart broke a second time when his grandmother stepped on the porch with tears running down her face, screaming for her daughter.

Looking at him, his grandmother said, "I already called for help, baby. The police and ambulance on the way. I don't wanna see you in cuffs, baby, so you and that girl need to get up out of here. I don't wanna see my great grandbaby around whatever you and yo' brothers about to do. But I tell you this, and you can tell them what I said. I don't wanna see any one of y'all until every motherfucka involved in my baby being hurt is dead, and God forbid she dies 'cause you motherfuckas better make them build a new cemetery, or all you motherfuckas are dead to me!"

Pooh was looking at his grandmother, stunned and really scared to speak until he heard the sirens growing closer. Snapping out of it, he called for Bailey while running toward the car. Before he got in, he looked at both his mother and grandmother, swearing he was going to fulfill his grandmother's wishes or die trying.

Chapter 24

Bronze was sitting in his cell, waiting for news of Two-Feet's demise from the "Guys" upstairs, as he had sent the greenlight as soon as the phone hung up. He really wanted to talk to Memphis to get confirmation from him, but he knew protocol, and Queen's word was just as good; wrong or right, Memphis would back up anything Queen said or did and simply chastise her behind closed doors if she made a bad call. But he would never give anybody the idea that they weren't on the same page about everything in public.

He was also thinking about the shit Queen had just said. Memphis made sure The Circle never really beefed with anybody, especially any of the heavyweights or local gangs, yet somebody with major balls or backing had to be behind the attempt on his house. There wasn't just any nigga who'd try a move like that, knowing how Memphis and his brothers got down. Not to mention, how would they know where he lived anyway?

Yeah, he knew Blacc had switched sides, but would he really be bold enough to go up against them in that form or way, especially after all the years they had grinded, fought side by side, and come up out of the struggle together? Shit, even he remembered when Mcmphis used to take Blacc to work—it was his first and only job—making sure he had money in his pocket before he left. Could Blacc really forget all that, just to try to take his place?

Then the shit about DJ and Wiz was even crazier. Wiz was supposed to be upstairs on the 5th floor (capital offenses), yet he was somehow free. Hell, he had even smashed one of the OT (out of town) niggas for speaking bad on his homies and was about to put the nigga on the door until a nigga he had grown up with came out of nowhere to vouch.

"Yeah, Wiz was out and had even sold him some work the week before he was indicted," he'd said. Hearing that and the news that DJ was with him and had work, let him know two things for sure. Memphis couldn't know, because there was no way he was giving either of them any work, especially DJ. The second thing was, they had to be hot, working for either the feds, DEA, or anybody else who wanted to see The Circle fall.

What had him perplexed was the timing of it all. Somebody had framed him for a body he knew he hadn't done, with multiple witnesses saying they were there to see it. Two-Feet, DJ, and Wiz were all growing tails, turning into rats. Blacc all of a sudden switched sides, when he and Memphis had been grooming Blacc and Pooh to take over for years.

He was trying to put the pieces of the puzzle together when Lil' Folks ran into his cell, saying he needed to see the news immediately.

Chapter 25

Queen was glad Key didn't ask any questions about the police surveillance sitting out front until they got into the backyard, and Key saw the mess the dogs had made.

"Oh, hell nawl," Key said, backing up. "I fuck with you and bro the long way, but I ain't fuckin' with no body parts. Shit, if the motherfuckas was still together, I'd even grab a shovel and help you dig their graves. But look at this shit, sis!" Key said, kicking a hand that was missing three fingers. "This looks like some shit straight out of a Michael Myers, Freddy Krueger movie!" Key yelled.

"I know, I know!" Queen said. "Hell, I had to wrestle with one of the dogs to get an arm back. Well, shit, I think it was an arm."

"Who the fuck are these niggas?" Key asked.

"Shit, I don't know," Queen honestly stated. "I was in the house, playing the game, when they called themselves, I guess, about to break in!"

"Even with all them police out front?" Key asked.

"Again, I don't know, sis, and honestly, I'm not about to play the fuckin' guessing game, trying to find out. I simply wanna get as much of this shit in a pile as I can so I can get it bagged up and get the fuck out of here."

"But what about all the blood, sis?" Key asked.

"Shit, the water hose over there, and I brought the bleach out with me when I put the dogs up. After that, I'm just gon' sprinkle the rest of the mulch that was left over on top of it until Memphis gets back to do whatever else."

Shaking her head, Key grabbed the mittens off the top of the grill and a bag to begin filling it. They were halfway done when Rosie suddenly appeared, throwing up when she saw both of the torsos that were laid side by side.

"What the fuck did y'all do?" Rosie asked, startling both of them.

"Them damn dogs," Queen said, leaving it at that.

"Why didn't you just leave it for bro to clean up?" Rosie asked, being her irritating, naive self, as usual.

"Because I don't have time to let one of them motherfuckas up front see this shit, and stop asking me questions I can't fuckin' answer. What you doing back anyway? We ain't spend all that money getting you into that art school for you to be ditching!" Queen said, looking at Rosie with a mug.

"No! I was on my way to school when Bob from Mommy's job texted me, asking was Mommy okay because she wasn't answering and didn't come in today. I tried to call her a bunch of times with it going straight to voicemail. Then, when I tried to call you, I didn't get an answer, and big bro told me anytime something seems wrong or I get nervous or scared, come home, so that's what I did!" Rosie said, on the brink of tears.

"Okay, okay, calm down!" Queen noticed Rosie was getting worked up. "Go get me one of those car covers so I can roll these things up," Queen said while kicking one of the torsos.

When they were done, Queen looked Rosie in the eyes, telling her she had to go to the store real quick and for her not to open the door or answer it for anybody.

Before Queen could get her purse, Rosie stopped her. "Hey, should I feed the dogs?"

Queen looked at her and smirked. "They already ate."

Rosie looked at the unopened bag of dog food and asked, "How?" She looked confused.

Queen laughed and said, "Because some people don't pay attention to the 'beware of dog' signs."

Queen was still laughing until Rosie pointed to the TV. "Look!"

Chapter 26

Toya doubled back after dropping Strip off on the block behind the house they had been parked across the street from. Even though Strip had a good plan, something in her gut and mind told her Strip was still gon' need her. Plus, he still owed her an explanation for what the fuck was going on, as well as whether she and her babies were truly safe. After this morning, she was low-key scared to even go home, so she didn't want to hear that shit about her catching up with him later.

Plus, she just wanted to see if his plan would work. She thought shit like that only happened in movies. So far, it seemed like it was working. She saw Strip creeping up the side of the house after apparently making it over both gates without setting off any alerts or alarms, but to her, that was the easy part. She wanted to see how he was gon' take out four people—two of them having their own guns—with only thirteen bullets.

Shit, God forbid he miss or get into a shootout because, if so, he was fucked. Plus, she didn't even know what she'd be able to do to help or save him. Rolling down her window so she could have a clear, unobstructed view—plus be able to hear—she was surprised to see Strip push off the house at normal speed, shooting one detective, then the other one, both in the head. She, and hopefully everybody else, barely heard the shots.

She was even more surprised and amazed at how calm and cool Strip looked. He wasn't yelling, jumping around, or anything, and he honestly just appeared to be having a normal conversation with the other two guys until they began to quickly strip.

She was astonished at how easy and fast everything seemed to happen until her attention was drawn to the back door of the Trackhawk being opened with someone pointing a gun out at Strip. Reacting without thinking, she threw the truck in gear, gunning it and screaming out Strip's name.

For his part, Strip saw DJ's eyes dart behind him with a slight smile forming on his face, which let him know shit was shifting out of his favor. Saying *fuck it*, he shot DJ between the eyes and was reaching out to grab Wiz to use as a shield when he heard rubber being burnt. Turning around, he was surprised to see Toya run her truck right into the Trackhawk, causing someone to fall out.

Seeing the threat, he shot the lil' nigga without thinking twice. He was getting the tape out of the dead detective's pocket when Wiz finally spoke. "Please don't, bro! At least let me tell my kids bye!"

Strip paused before emptying the rest of the clip into Wiz's face. "They straight. They'll never talk rodent talk!"

Chapter 27

Jimmy hadn't heard from Memphis, but he was on the first flight out of Music City (Nashville, TN), after hearing his big sister—his only sister—Whitney, had been shot. He still couldn't believe that none of the kids called to tell him, which had him wondering if they even knew. Most importantly, what the hell was going on? After the hospital called him, he checked the newsfeed while waiting to board his flight and could tell that it hadn't been some random shit or her simply being caught at the wrong place at the wrong time type shit.

No. The action had been brought straight to her doorstep, which was weird, seeing all the trouble Memphis had gone through to make sure no one knew where his mother lived. Jimmy shook his head, remembering all the back-and-forth flights he had to take to secure the purchase, with the boys smiling the whole time, not caring how much extra they were spending on all the trips. They just wanted their mother to be safe.

He thought about it… Somebody had to be an idiot to go after their mother without getting all of the boys first. Nothing in this world, including the undertaker, was about to stop them from wreaking havoc on not just the city, but the state.

Jimmy was closing his eyes for a quick nap when he suddenly remembered something. Last week, Memphis called him, wanting him to look into something, as well as invest in a new stock he heard about and a few properties, but he was busy and told him to call back next week. Next week was today, and Memphis hadn't called, something that had never happened before. He was a real nerd when it came to promptness, especially concerning business, and he simply would not have missed his appointment, even if the house were on fire.

Something was definitely up; he just wasn't sure if he wanted to know what it was. He was the oddball and black sheep of the family, as everybody besides his niece—and even she'd had a slight run-in—had been in the game one way or another. He had his wife, kids, career, and childhood friends around whom he had created a life, so he didn't get involved with anything from the other side of the tracks besides the occasional advice, and even that had slowed up now that everyone was grown and free to make their own choices and decisions.

Plus, with his two boys in sports, he had little time for concentrating on anything else anyway. He just hated that his sister had gotten caught up in whatever the boys had going on, and prayed she made it, for everybody's sake. Even his…

Chapter 28

Getting out of the clinic turned into a mission in itself. After finding whoever the lil' nigga was some clothes, they bumped into a slight problem when the head doctor demanded triple the normal cost for treating both Stacy and the youngster, due to his staff being assaulted or literally knocked the fuck out. The money itself wasn't the problem; it was convincing the other doctor not to press charges, which ended up even worse, being that Dee wasn't a fan of any type of police shit. Plus, Dee felt the youngster was in the right. He was afraid of hospitals, too, so he totally understood how the youngster felt, being woken up by a white stranger talking about cutting him.

"Shit, at least the youngster only knocked him out!" Dee said. "Shit, I would've killed his ass!" And no one doubted it by the look on Dee's face.

So when the doctor jumped up, talking about calling the police, Dee dropped him and put his gun in the doctor's mouth, asking him if he was sure. With the doctor crying, shaking his head left to right, Dee reached into his pocket, handing the doctor his whole knot, simply telling the doctor to take the money and a two-to-three-day vacation and forget that he'd ever seen any of them.

They bumped into their next problem when they attempted to call Queen to let her know they were on their way back, only to be told that Queen was unavailable and to stay where they were until further notice. Stacy, not liking what she heard, snatched the phone, thinking she would have better luck, only to realize she was talking to Rosie—on the house phone at that. Those were two things that never happened and didn't make sense, and if things couldn't get worse or more confusing than that, while they were helping the youngster in the car, two unmarked vehicles pulled in front of the clinic, letting out several clearly law-enforcement type motherfuckas.

Knowing then and there wasn't the time for a shoot-out, they got into both vehicles, leaving quietly, with Slim and Dee closely following Stacy in case anyone had seen Stacy's car or tag number.

Chapter 29

Bailey didn't know what Pooh was thinking, nor had she ever seen him this mad or upset. After leaving his mom's house, he had driven straight to Family Dollar, telling her to go in and buy as many prepaid phones as she could. Coming out, she noticed he had changed shirts as well as put on his bulletproof vest.

She went to open the passenger door, but the window came down, Pooh telling her to get in the back. She looked at him confusedly until she looked down and saw the bag of guns sitting on the seat. Twisting her lips, she was about to cuss his ass out, but she thought better of it after looking at his eyes. It looked like he was possessed or something.

She jumped in the back, and he had already put the car in reverse before she could even close her door. She went to ask him a question, but before the words were out of her mouth, the sounds of Young Boy filled the car, so she just sat back, not wanting to upset him more. No more than five or six minutes had passed before she noticed he had pulled into an apartment complex with a lot of men standing in front of one building.

Without saying anything or giving her a heads up, Pooh got out, shooting what she later would find out was called a Drako. She watched him go through two circle clips thingies—or 'drans', she would later be told they were called—stepping over dead bodies and clearing out the parking lot before getting back in the car as if nothing had happened.

As they left, she thought he would've been speeding or trying to get away from the area as quickly as possible. Instead, he drove like he was simply going to the store, even when he jumped on the interstate, getting off two exits later on Camelback Road.

Pulling up to a nondescript building, she watched him grab an AR-type rifle, get out of the car, walk up to the door, and knock. As soon as the door opened, Pooh began shooting as he walked in. It seemed like forever, but it was maybe only two minutes. The door burst open with a big ass dude running out and falling over his own feet. Pooh stepped out, changed clips, and stood over the dude before emptying the new clip into the guy's body, damn near shredding him into pieces.

Getting back into the car, Pooh sang along to Lil' Durk's "Risky" while jumping back on the E-way, heading south. Jumping off on 7th Street, he stopped at what he and his brothers called the 'don't ask, don't tell' motel, and told her to grab a room. When she came out, he handed her the bag of phones, telling her to activate all of them, and he would be back in less than an hour.

Looking at him, she noticed he had a sad, faraway look on his face, so she knew whatever he was about to do was deeper than anything prior. It was confirmed when he kissed her palm and told her he loved her and to let his brothers know he was going to Park South. Knowing how it was set up, she asked him if he was going to the front or the back, and she could've fainted when, before pulling off, he said, "Both…"

Chapter 30

Twist was in a world of bliss and pussy between the thick ass chocolate bunny thighs. After being checked earlier by Queen, she had gone out to get her something to blow on and drink, wondering if Memphis was gon' snap on her ass or trip about her coming off slick to Queen or not. The truth of the matter was, she didn't like Queen, because Queen had honestly come out of nowhere and was given rank and power simply because she was Memphis' wife.

Queen hadn't thugged with them. She wasn't with them in the early days when they were breaking into cars and shit just to have enough for a bag and a bottle or kicking in people's doors, hoping that the people weren't as broke or fucked up as they were. She hadn't been shot at, beaten up by different crews, or had to put in the type of work that each of them had. Yet somehow, what she said went.

Twist was thinking all of those things, coming out of the Wal-Mart liquor store, when she noticed this high-yellow, ugly motherfucka parked next to her that was talking crazy as fuck to someone sitting in their car, crying. She was shaking her head, laughing, until he started talking shit about how dark and ugly the girl was, which definitely was a no-go for her, seeing that she had been picked on most of her life growing up—not just because of the color of her skin, but also because she was a real nigga trapped inside of a female's body.

Nearing her car, she cracked a joke about how all yellow motherfuckas ain't pretty either and was about to get in her car and leave until dude got slick, telling her to suck his dick.

She would have let it slide, had he simply said fuck her or maybe even called her a bitch. But telling her to suck his coward ass dick when she knew hers was bigger than his was something she just couldn't let slide, which was like music to her ears, based on how she was feeling.

Pulling out her .45, she ran back around the car, striking the dude across his head before shoving her pole into his mouth. Looking into the car, she saw the prettiest dark-skinned bitch she had seen in a while and got even more upset, thinking about how this hoe ass, ugly motherfucka had probably used and abused her. She was about to pull the trigger, not giving a fuck where she was, until the girl asked her not to because he wasn't worth it, and asked her if she would simply give her a ride home.

That was four hours ago, and neither one of them was tired or bored yet. Hearing her phone ring, Twist was about to ignore the call until the thought of it being Queen or Memphis made her reluctantly grab it. Answering it without looking at the screen, she was about to hang up when she heard it was neither of them.

Then the words, "It wasn't us," graced her ears.

Looking at her phone, she noticed she had several text messages from motherfuckas she wouldn't imagine calling her phone, and they all said the same thing.

Chapter 31

Queen had given Rosie Key's number, telling her to only give it to the boys if they called and to simply say she was unavailable and take messages for anyone else calling—because she would call regularly to check the messages or to see if anybody had called—so she was royally pissed the fuck off, walking into the hospital, when Key tried handing her the phone, saying it was Twist. Not taking it, she told Key to tell her she was busy and would get back to her momentarily.

After getting directions to her mother-in-law's room, she raced off the elevator, only to be stopped by the police telling her that Ms. Whitney's family didn't want any visitors. Insulted, she pushed the cop's hands off her.

"I am family, bitch!" she screamed, only causing more officers to rush over. Seeing her distraught, a middle-aged Black doctor came over, asking what the problem was. Turning toward him, she told the doctor who she was and asked if her mother-in-law was okay.

Thinking the doctor was about to lead her to Ms. Whitney, she pushed away from the officers, only to be stopped by the doctor telling her Ms. Whitney was alive but in a coma, and her mother, Ms. Rhonda, didn't want her daughter seen or bothered by anyone.

Thinking she'd heard wrong, she asked the doctor to repeat that, only to be told the same thing. She got even more pissed off when she asked the doctor if she could please speak with Ms. Rhonda, only for the doctor to walk off and return and say that Ms. Rhonda didn't want to speak or have any visitors. She was about to either bribe the doctor or threaten him when Key handed her the phone, saying it was Strip and her mother. Walking away angrily, she snatched the phone.

"Speak," she said, trying to imitate Memphis, only to be halted by her mother's labored breathing as she told her she was hurt. They were currently in a high-speed chase, Strip saying the truck wasn't gonna make it much longer because of the damage it sustained when she drove it into the Trackhawk. Speedwalking through the hospital, she asked where they were and dropped her head when her mom told her they were in Chandler. She knew, with all the big stores and outlets out that way, there was no way that they were going to make it all the way back to North Phoenix, an hour and a half trip, in a chase with a damaged truck.

Thinking quickly, she remembered that Butch, Stacy's father, worked that way. She told them to hold on and called on three-way, praying, unlike most people, that he would answer a number he didn't know. Hearing him answer the second ring, she could've jumped for joy. Not saying too much, she told him her mom and Strip were in trouble out that way and needed a lift back to Phoenix.

He made her sigh in relief when he said his shift had just started, and he couldn't leave, but the keys were in his truck, and they could take it as long as they got there and could pick him up after work. Clicking back over, she had him tell Strip where he worked and felt like a job well done when Strip said, "I'm less than five minutes away."

Chapter 32

Bronze was sitting in the holding cell, holding an ice pack to the back of his head, wondering what the fuck was really going on, as well as how they were going to try to hang him next. He knew he'd probably be able to beat the assault-on-staff case or charge, since the pastor had seen everything that occurred. Everything else was a mystery. At this point, though, he really didn't give a fuck. He just needed to get to a phone to check in and check on his God Mama to see how his brothers were. Even though they weren't blood, their bond-in-love couldn't have been thicker or stronger, and he loved each of them—even Pooh—like he had come out of Ms. Whitney's womb with them.

Plus, he knew they would have to call the National Guard in, not to stop, only slow the brothers down for what happened to Ms. Whitney, which was another reason he needed to talk to Memphis ASAP, or at least Queen. He knew they were the only two people the other brothers would listen to. Not to mention, he needed to warn them about the active investigation they were under. Shit, Memphis, being himself, probably already knew and was building a defense for it.

He just didn't want or need any more shit to pop off, as he was already confused. Coming out of his cell to see the news, he was bumrushed by the CRT team that was asking and really trying to pin Two-Feet's murder on him. Seeing the news, he asked them to give him a minute to see what was going on with his mom. Forgetting who he was, they tried muscling him, but it did not go the way they thought it would; several other inmates got involved.

Then, after being harassed by CRT, he came back to the dorm to a stand-off between him and two different gangs. Pooh had apparently gone on a killing spree, hitting both gangs back-to-back. If that wasn't enough shit to deal with, CRT was breaking the baby riot up in the dorm. He held rank in the jail for The Circle and supported and rode for the decisions any of them made.

Before he could finish dealing with that, he was escorted upstairs to an interview room, where he was met by two detectives, concerning all the killings that were taking place. Even though the streets knew what was going on, nobody stepped forward to say shit yet. He just didn't know how long that would last, as rats always seemed to find a way to squeak. All the police knew was that a bunch of shit had popped off right after Ms. Whitney was shot.

After those two detectives stepped out of the room, two different detectives walked in, asking about Strip, as well as the two detectives and two informants who were found slain. Bronze, puzzled, couldn't help but laugh at first, thinking they were joking, and then he was confused as fuck when he realized they were serious. He couldn't see Memphis or Queen sanctioning that unless it was absolutely necessary, which meant shit was worse than he thought.

His refusing to say anything at all only pissed the two detectives off more, causing them to tell the COs to show him a lil' love on the way back to his cell, which would have been all bad, had the paster not been on the scene to inform him of Ms. Whitney's condition. He was ready to get back to his dorm so he could release some of his frustration on any motherfucka that had shit to say about any moves The Circle was making. Then he was placed in the holding cell and given an ice pack for his head, being informed that his lawyer was there to see him.

Chapter 33

They had been driving around for almost an hour, really just going in circles, before Stacy pulled into a no-name bread, non-descript motel, got out, and went in to get two ground-floor, connecting rooms. She knew that was what her brother would do. On top of that, she knew she needed a hot shower and some rest.

Although she didn't know everything that was going on, she could tell something was very, very wrong; the fact that Dee and Slim were there instead of one or all of her brothers said a lot. It also had her both worried and concerned, seeing that she hadn't talked to or heard from either of them since before she left, something that had never happened before.

Not wanting to cry or panic, she sat there for a moment, taking a deep breath, trying to get her thoughts together. As of right then, everything was just a blur and confusing as fuck, hell, even the guy she was thinking about sharing a room with. She still didn't even know his name. She just didn't wanna be alone, and the thought of sharing a room with someone who worked for her brother was weird to even think about. Her brother had always told her to get a man who was his own boss, not a worker or follower.

Finding the room was easy, but she could tell that the others needed some rest, too, by how slow they were. Any other time, they'd usually beat her out of the car. Now they were just sitting there, looking just as lost and confused as she felt.

Seeing her get out and open her room door, Dee jumped out to help get the youngster in the room, and he noticed all the blood covering the driver's seat. Immediately, he knew that they had to get rid of the car. There was no way it would go unnoticed, and second, anyone seeing it besides a nigga would most definitely report it to the police. It looked like someone had died in there. After calling Slim over to show him, he walked into the room, asking Stacy for her keys, telling her they had to toe tag her car.

Stacy was reaching for her keys when Slim walked into the room to ask if she'd had a chance to make the drop, which caused everyone to stare at her. Shaking her head no brought more questions and confused looks than she could handle. Getting upset, she tossed her keys to Slim, telling him to get everything out of the car while she tried to get in touch with someone again.

Shaking his head at all the back-and-forth shit, Chauncey sat down, leaning back on the other bed, thinking about his own problems and predicament when he saw both Slim and Dee walk in with packages he knew hadn't been in the car. His eyes almost popped out of his head when he noticed what they were. He closed his eyes and opened them again, willing what he was seeing to disappear. Just the thought of what could be made would have every jack boy in a thousand-mile radius ready to kill everyone in the room, including him.

Chapter 34

Strip knew he couldn't take Toya to a hospital, as by now, her picture was probably already all over the news. It was crazy how fast everything had fallen apart, and as bad as he wanted to be mad at Toya for not listening to him, he was actually glad she hadn't. There was a good chance he would be dead if she hadn't shown back up.

Hell, he still couldn't believe how fucked up his luck was. How the hell was he to know that DJ's rat ass was working for the Maricopa PD and under surveillance by the DEA? Shit, he really wished he could go back and kill the stupid motherfucka again, and he really would've taken his time to do it.

Who the fuck would've ever thought that the crackers had a fuckin' drone up over them the whole time? Shit, thinking about it pissed him off again. Shit like that fucked up the whole game. How the fuck could a nigga sit back and get money when, at any given time, a fuckin' drone could be in the sky, watching without anyone knowing it?

Looking over at Toya, he had the urge to lean over to kiss her because she was holding on and handling shit like a G. He knew killers that had been shot in the shoulder and cried like a bitch, yet there lil' mama was, not only talking shit to him about his driving, but also pissed the fuck off about them having to ditch her new truck like that was the worst of their problems. He still couldn't believe that, after running her truck into the other one, she hopped out to grab a gun, or that she hung out the window, busting that bitch at their pursuers, not knowing at first or caring after she found out that it was the police.

If nothing else happened in life, that was some of the most gangsta shit he had ever seen from a female. Her getting shot in the shoulder was some fluke shit, and even that was crazy, as he still hadn't seen her drop or shed a single tear. All she kept talking about was getting a bottle to dull the pain and something about breaking a nail while trying to use the lil' ass phone. Yeah, Toya was definitely a rider, and if they ever made it to somewhere safe to chill, he was gon' get all up in her business because motherfuckas like that didn't just wake up pretending to be gangsta. That shit was bred into them from birth, so he wanted to know her whole fuckin' story.

His thoughts were interrupted when Toya told him he needed to get to South Phoenix as soon as possible. After asking where, he was even more confused when she said the lil' motel on 7th Street.

Chapter 35

Jimmy landed at Sky Harbor International Airport in South Phoenix and was both angry and surprised to find no one waiting for him. He had left several messages for Rosie, including his flight number and the time he was scheduled to land. There had never been a time when no one had been there to get him, or at least a town car taking him to somebody's house if one of the boys wasn't available to pick him up. Hell, even his niece had been there once, happy to show off her baby Benz that Memphis and the boys had gotten her when she graduated.

Sure, he was a civilian, not involved in anything the boys had going on, but they always made sure he was safe and protected in their city, where they seemed to have many enemies. Hell, thinking about what had just happened to his sister made him speedwalk to a cab, not wanting to be standing out in the open for too long. Jumping into the cab, he told the driver to take him to Banner Health, then sat back and closed his eyes. Before he could even process the fact that he was in the back of a cab, the driver knocked on the window, saying they were there. It only took about seven minutes.

Getting off the elevator on his sister's floor, he would've thought he was on the wrong floor, had he not seen several officers standing around. What he didn't see was any of the kids or other knuckleheads that he knew would have been posted on the floor—police presence or not.

Before the police could stop him, he saw his mom run out of the room, chasing a little boy he suspected was Lil' Pooh.

When he scooped the boy up, his mom saw him, seemed to pause like a deer caught in headlights, turned, and walked back into the room. The police, seeing this, backed up, letting him pass.

Tickling the lil' boy, he asked him where he thought he was going and was shocked to hear him say, "Nigga, put me down! I don't know you!" That caused several of the officers who were close enough to hear it to laugh.

Walking into his sister's room, he wasn't ready for what he saw, nor the confrontation he saw brewing on his mother's face.

Chapter 36

Pooh had lost the element of surprise and had a feeling he was at his end. After jumping out of the car, wetting up the back streets, he had tricked the fronts, making them think he rode for them, just to get in to see the big homie Skitz, who really had shit on lock for the Locs. True enough, he didn't have any smoke or problems with Skitz, and he lowkey fucked with him.

At the same time, Skitz and Memphis had bumped heads in the past when Skitz tried to play Memphis at a dice game, not knowing who he was. It ended with Memphis shooting Skitz and killing Trae, Skitz's bodyguard. Even though they squashed it, the word was Skitz still felt some type of way about it and had gotten drunk a few times, making threats that made their way back to The Circle.

That wasn't lost on Skitz, which was why his two shooters were still in the room with them, especially after hearing the rampage Pooh had been on. Nobody really knew what the fuck was going on, which was why everybody was on edge.

Pooh, feeling the tension and like he already had the upper hand since he wasn't dead yet, looked Skitz in the eyes and said, "I don't really like talking with hoes in the room, but since I see you need some reassurance, tell me it wasn't y'all that got my moms laid out in the hospital, and I'ma let them two bitches behind you live…"

Skitz, not liking the disrespect but knowing the youngster had to have a death wish or something up his sleeves to come into his hood—his house—talking like that, laughed to ease the tension. "Nigga, when I send a hit, my hittas bury shit, and we definitely don't go after harmless people. No disrespect, but the fact that she still breathing should let you know it wasn't us."

Pooh, not liking the answer and how it was said, still felt like he needed to send a message. "So, um, what's this shit I been hearing about you not liking how my brother slumped ya manz?"

Skitz, seeing what the youngster was trying to do, laughed because, although he admired the youngster, he lowkey felt like his gangsta was being tested. He stood up. "What? You think because you got that blue rag hanging around yo' neck, you safe in here, nigga? Huh? Because I'll bury yo' lil' ass and go to war with all yo' brothers and y'all lil' ass circle!" he barked.

Pooh cracked up, laughing, trying to remember how many shells he had left in the FN because Skitz was the second nigga in less than twenty-four hours that had said some fuck shit about burying him, and he wasn't having it or letting it slide.

Chapter 37

Twist called Razor, their big OG, after trying to call everyone countless times. She even called the jail and left a message telling them it was a family emergency and for Bronze to call his baby sister after trying to call his baby cell phone, but it was repeatedly going straight to voicemail.

She couldn't believe Pooh had singlehandedly waged war against everyone in the city that they had ever beefed with without warning her. She knew niggas were pussy, and they picked and chose, so they would come after her first because she was a female or because they would think she was the weakest link. They were going to be in for a big surprise and a world of trouble, though, because she wasn't sparing anyone or letting *anything* slide. Shit, she had worked too hard to build up her name and reputation not to go all in now. Shit, this was where it was really about to matter.

She called Razor because he was their OG; he had been around, and not only had unlimited hitters, but he also had unlimited love and access around the city. Plus, he could get to the bottom of whatever the fuck was going on faster than anybody. On top of that, Razor knew motherfuckas that knew motherfuckas and could tell them exactly where their enemy was without having to search high and low for them.

That was how she found out that, at that very moment, Pooh was inside Skitz's house, possibly about to do something really dumb. The word was, the motherfuckas they were really looking for were laid back in Mesa, laughing, thinking shit was sweet. Razor, peeping what was up, hit Skitz's people up, letting them know they were five or six minutes away, and if anything popped off before he got there, he would consider it disrespect.

Twist, knowing how hot-headed Pooh could be, knew that Razer's threat may not be enough to stop him, especially if he was already on go. So, she called Key's phone again, demanding that Queen get her ass on the phone. Everyone knew Memphis and Queen were the only two people living who could tell the brothers what to do, and she even felt some type of way about that because she had known all of them way longer than Queen. Shit, she still couldn't understand how the fuck their bond had gotten so tight or how everybody just jumped when Queen spoke.

Hell, if anything, she was supposed to be the first lady or the queen in The Circle, seeing that she had been there since birth and their start, yet motherfuckas only did what she told them if they knew Memphis or Bronze had put her over whatever project or mission. Even now, she was pissed off because she had directly given both Slim and Dee something to do, yet they hadn't been seen, nor had she heard from them all fuckin' day. On top of that, no one had answered or returned any of her calls besides motherfuckas outside of their circle, and that was only to either cop duces or make idle ass threats that she was itching to see about.

On top of all that, Blacc had stopped by two weeks ago to pick up the bread for the plug and re-up money, yet she hadn't heard from the plug about where she needed to have her girls to pick up the next shipment, which was also weird as fuck but was something that had happened before. That was why she hadn't jumped to conclusions and run to Memphis yet, especially with everything on his plate, trying to tap into the Dakotas. Her thoughts came to a screeching halt when she saw Strip hop out of a familiar-looking truck with two bangers in his hands.

Chapter 38

Queen had a hundred things on her mind, coming out of Target after getting some new prepaid phones. The last thing she expected to hear was Key say, "I think we're being followed." Knowing better than to look back, she asked her why and which car. Seeing the car with the tint and rims on it let her know it wasn't the boys, and if it wasn't the boys, and they were indeed following them, then the car meant them no good, especially with everything that had happened so far.

Hating that she didn't have a pole on her, she told Key to hit the E-Way to see how bold their pursuers were. If she could make it to Glendale, whoever was following them was fucked, as nobody in Glendale would allow a hair on her head to be touched without her or Memphis's consent. She slightly relaxed, seeing that the car kept going without getting on the E-way with them and laughed, cranking Glorilla's new shit to the max until Key tapped her, motioning behind them.

Leaning slightly forward, she looked in the sideview mirror, seeing that not only was the car back, but it wasn't even trying to hide this time. It was glued to their ass, right on the bumper. She looked at Key confusedly, seeing her get off on Indian School until the music cut off with Slim's voice coming over the radio speakers.

"What's up, baby?"

"Oh, nothing, love. Me and Queen was trying to shop until I noticed I had a new bumper sticker!"

"Oh yeah?" he asked.

"Yeah, baby, a dark-green one!"

"Damn, where y'all at?"

"Three minutes from the old restaurant," she said.

"Ohh, okay. Well, look, I gotta go. Slide by the restaurant. I'm about to place a order."

"I love you, babe," she cooed.

"I love yo' ass too. Now bye, girl."

Queen was about to cuss Key the fuck out, watching her hit the end button, wondering how the fuck she could be so joyful about some fuckin' food when they had a big ass problem on their hands. Then she noticed they were by the old cook-up spot that they had converted into a dice spot. Knowing she could easily get a pole from anyone there, she told Key to turn in, hoping someone would be there at this time of day.

"What the fuck!" she screamed, watching Key pass it until what sounded like a band started up behind them.

She looked back, and the car that had been following them was barely moving, blood all over the windshield and what appeared to be flames coming from the hood. Queen cracked up, laughing, until she looked over and saw Key slightly trembling.

Chapter 39

Bronze walked out of the visit with his attorney, wishing for a drink, a blunt, hell, even a fuckin' perc to try to wrap his mind around everything that was going on. His lawyer had blessed him with the good news first. Four of the six fake ass witnesses on his murder case had been killed, and the other two had contacted his lawyer voluntarily to write and sign affidavits saying that they were paid to lie.

It should've gotten the case tossed out. However, the D.A. was playing hardball, refusing to drop the case, and had even filed additional charges against him, including threatening and intimidating, tampering with evidence, and another murder case that took place while he was locked up, plus an assault with serious bodily injury on a correctional officer, and he would be arraigned for all of them in the morning.

Although his lawyer promised him he was going to be able to beat them all, he was still going to have to sit, as the judge wasn't going to change his mind about not giving him a bond. On top of that, even though the charges were frivolous, he needed an additional sixty thousand dollars to represent him on them, or he could take his chances with a court-appointed lawyer—a public pretender that may have or may not have owed the D.A. a favor or two.

Bronze knowing that either way, he was getting fucked, agreed to get the lawyer the money. At least that way, he knew what the outcome would be. Plus, no price was worth his freedom from the dick heads that were trying to take it. He would just have to holler at Memphis and break everything down to him.

The lawyer's next words froze him. "Oh yeah. Your uncle Ace is upset with you and your brother, too. He said he always knew you would stand on your own two feet like a man, but just because you locked up, bills don't stop." Reading between the lines, Bronze immediately understood what was being said. He just didn't understand the connection or how long he had. Trying not to show his true feelings, he said, "Ohh, did he say when it was due or how much it was?"

Staring him in his eyes, the lawyer said, "No, nor did I inquire either. He did say you had his number and that you could call at any time from anywhere. Though, me being your lawyer, I would advise the sooner, the better." He closed his briefcase before walking out of the room, not knowing or caring how heavy of a load he had just dropped on him.

As their plug, Ace was nothing to be played with or taken lightly, and just the fact that he was able to send him a message through his attorney let him know that he was also aware of everything that was going on. He just hoped no lines had been crossed that couldn't be erased.

When he walked back on his tier, the DO shouted that he had a family emergency and needed to call his baby sister. He picked up the phone, about to call Stacy, until the D.O.'s words replayed in his head. Had he simply said sister, he would've called Stacy, but by saying baby sister, he was referring to Twist, as his two older sisters, Shey and Lanetta, would've never called if something was wrong. They would've simply popped up, no matter what time of day it was, demanding to see him, even acting a donkey if they were denied.

Plus, Stacy was like Ms. Whitney, always over-protective of all the boys, like she was their mom, and she never would've referred to herself as a baby in any manner, so it had to be Twist, his baby sister, as all the boys referred to her, even though she was older than some of them. Hanging up the phone, he cursed under his breath, dialing her number, wondering what the fuck had happened.

Chapter 40

Dee and Slim had driven around the lil' city, seeing that it was more hood than they first realized. Although they first thought about torching the car, they changed their minds. They knew it wouldn't take investigators long to find one of the VIN numbers and trace the car back to them, no matter how badly it burned. Unlike old cars with only one VIN number on the dashboard, new cars had them all over, and once they ran it, it would raise more red flags and unwanted attention than they needed. Instead, they found a self-service car wash, scrubbed the seats and floorboards as much as they could, and left it running, knowing it would be gone in a matter of minutes.

Slim was still caught up on the phone call with his wife, Key. Yeah, living the life he lived, he prepared her for every scenario he could possibly think of, including the one they just executed, about what to do if she was ever followed or thought that she was in danger. And he was glad he had, as his homies told him that she definitely was on point. Upon looking into the car they lit up, several different kinds of guns were found inside.

He couldn't believe some shit like that had popped off with Key. Everybody knew his wife may've talked that gangster shit, but in reality, she wasn't living like that at all. Shit, she went to work faithfully—five, sometimes six days of every week—and was at every child event each of their six kids had, including the birthday parties of every kid in their neighborhood, so he couldn't even imagine how she was taking what had just happened. He just hoped Queen was sensitive to the fact and helped her get through it.

Then his thoughts turned dark, wondering who the fuck would try him like that, or Memphis, as everyone knew Memphis would rather anyone try him than Queen; trying her was like trying him twice. Then Key was like Memphis's big sister, so they were actually trying him all the way around, something that had never happened before, so he was ready to get back to Phoenix to put his own work in.

He had to really demonstrate and let everybody know his wife was not to be fucked with, like bro's weren't. Even though he protected her this time, he needed her to know he loved his family more than anything, and they would always be safe and protected.

His thoughts were interrupted by Dee pointing out several plays that were being made in plain sight. Like, it was amazing how niggas weren't even trying to hide what the fuck they were doing. They even watched a motherfucka shooting up while sitting at a bus stop while waiting to get their food from Popeyes.

Dee, being Dee, wanted to get some Zah to blow on plus see what everything was hitting for, so he jumped out to holler at a couple of niggas while Slim walked into Family Dollar to get everybody some hygiene shit and something to throw on until they could get to a mall or some shit. Meeting back up, Dee was all smiles the whole way back until they walked in the room and saw the youngster fuckin' with the work with his gun in his right hand…

Chapter 41

Strip moved as quickly as possible. After getting to the room, verifying that DoorDash was going to deliver everything Bailey needed to patch Toya up, he ran every stop sign, taking the back streets to Park South, hoping like hell he wasn't too late to save his lil' brother. Knowing his brother banged to the left, he hit the back streets first, knowing Pooh would've tried to kill every Blood that was out and about that day. His thoughts were confirmed by not seeing anyone outside. Heading back to the front, he passed Bailey's car, which was riddled with bullet holes. Not seeing any police presence let him know Pooh hadn't been in the car when it was shot up.

Before making it back to Southern, he saw about ten or fifteen niggas standing guard around Skitz's house. Knowing niggas were always outside but never on point like that, Strip threw Butch's truck in park and hopped out with tools in both hands, ready to go to work. Then he heard Twist calling his name. Turning around, he saw Twist and his childhood friend Razor telling him to wait.

Thinking about the shit with Wiz that, at once upon a time, had been both of their friends, reminded him of the tape in his pocket. It also made him ponder how Razor was gon' take it, being that Wiz and Razor had actually eaten off the same spoon and fork growing up, seeing as they grew up living next door to each other with their parents getting high together, which forced them into the streets before he even stepped off the porch with them.

Razor, seeing the crazed look in Strip's eyes, let him know that his friend was in battle mode, something he had seen countless times growing up with his partner. Trying to calm him down, he said, "Strip, it's alright, bro. I already made the call to let Skitz and everybody else in that house know if anything pop off, or if Pooh get hurt, it's up until every one of us—or them—is dead!"

Strip nodded, moving forward, not really giving a fuck what Razor said. Pooh was his baby brother, and he would be damned if he had to tell his mother, grandmother, or other brother that something happened to Pooh, especially if he was this close. So he caught the first nigga smirking off guard when he upped both poles at him, asking, "Where the fuck is my brother, since you think something funny?"

Everybody else in the yard stood frozen, not knowing what to do since Skitz had sent word out that nobody was to up or draw unless he told them to.

"In the house, nigga!" the youngster said, staring Strip in the eyes, not showing an ounce of fear.

Strip, knowing now wasn't the time or place, lowered his gun, telling the youngster to show him. He was caught off guard when the youngster mugged him with a scowl on his face, saying, "Fuck you!"

Worried about Pooh, Strip was about to shoot the youngster in his face to let everybody know he was serious until Skitz stepped on the porch, motioning for him, Razor, and Twist to follow him inside.

They all slightly relaxed when they walked in and saw Pooh standing with his back against a wall, taking a shot with his pole in his other hand.

Chapter 42

Jimmy was angrier than he had ever been. Seeing his big sister—really, his second mother, as she had raised him— hooked up to all the tubes and machines made him question whether there was really a God or not. He didn't understand how something like this, this bad, could happen to someone so loveable.

Sure, she wasn't innocent, as no one in life was, but as far as he knew, she had never even held a gun, let alone shot one or anybody. Yeah, he had heard about several incidents where she had stabbed abusive boyfriends, hell, even once when she had stabbed Memphis through his hand after he snatched the belt out of hers. But to see her like this was heartbreaking. He had watched her help countless people, even taking food out of her freezer and refrigerator to help people she didn't even know.

His thoughts were interrupted by Lil' Pooh asking his mama, "Who is this white boy, and why is he in our room, crying?"

Ms. Rhonda, trying not to cry herself, grabbed Lil' Pooh, telling him to hush, but Lil' Pooh, being a terrible toddler, raised his little voice to say, "Hey, white boy, who is you, and why you in my grandma room, crying like a punk?"

Jimmy only shook his head, seeing all of his nephews in the little boy, so he tried to smile. "Yo' uncle, lil' nigga, and you better watch yo' mouth around my mama!"

Before Lil' Pooh could respond, Ms. Rhonda exploded. "Ohh, now I'm yo' mama again, huh? You come in here crying like you all tore up, seeing your sister like this, but ain't called or been to see us in years. Hell, this lil' boy in my arms don't even know who the fuck you are, but you looking at me like I'm the one to blame for this shit. You telling him to watch how he talk in front of yo' mama, but when was the last time you called or even spoke to me? Huh?"

Before Ms. Rhonda could continue, the door opened with an officer sticking his head in the door asking, "Is everything alright?"

Angered by everything he was seeing, as well as the words his mom had just said, Jimmy snapped.

"Yeah! Matter of fact, why the fuck are y'all even here, just fuckin' standing around and shit, when whoever the fuck did this to my sister is still out and about?"

The officer turned beet red, trying to close the door, when Jimmy stormed toward it, snatching it. "Matter of fact, all y'all get the fuck away from my sistah's room. We don't fuck with the police!"

The head detective tried stepping forward to say something about it being an open investigation, only to be cut off by Jimmy.

"I ain't got no rap for you, and anything else you wanna say or ask need to be directed to our lawyer. Now bounce!"

Seeing the room door open, the detective thought it was Ms. Rhonda coming to check the dude or tell them they could stay, but he was surprised when he saw it was Lil' Pooh. He dropped his head, walking off, mumbling.

Then the lil' boy said, "You heard my uncle! We don't fuck with the police! Now bounce!"

Grabbing Lil' Pooh, Jimmy walked back into his sister's room, addressing his mom for the first time in years. "We can deal with all that later. Here and now is not the place for all that shit. Now, where the fuck is everybody, what happened to my sister, and why is it just you and this baby in this room by y'all selves with no security?"

Chapter 43

Rosie was sick and tired of answering the house phone, as well as steadily answering the same dumb ass questions over and over and over again, sometimes to the same damn people. Like, what the fuck didn't anybody get? No, neither her brother nor her sister was there. No, she didn't know where they were or when they would be back, and no, she didn't have their numbers or a way to reach them. Even if she did, she wouldn't give or tell it to them, because if they wanted them to have it, they would've given it out themselves.

Hell, she was being nice by asking them if they wanted to leave a message, and even took the time to write their name and message if they left one. On top of that, she still hadn't heard from her mother, which was "Crae Crae" to her. Her mom was her best friend, and they always talked, no matter if they were at school, work, or wherever. So, for the whole day to pass by without even a text message from her mama was disturbing, especially given the fact that her mom hadn't gone to work that day—unless one of her lil' boyfriends had popped up from out of town or something.

Yeah, that has to be it, she thought and really wished Queen hadn't been so dramatic about not answering the door or leaving the house, or she would've popped up at her mom's house like "What' up?" She laughed at herself in the mirror, throwing up the peace sign.

She was searching for something to watch on TV when all at once, all the dogs started growling, followed by a loud boom from the kitchen area. Jumping up, she was about to follow the dogs to where the noise had come from until she heard what sounded like a loud slap, followed by one of the dogs whining loudly. She knew that whatever was in the house had to be big as fuck to hurt one of their dogs. She reached into the closet, grabbing Queen's shotgun with both hands, just as Memphis had taught her.

Seeing that it was already loaded, she stepped out of her room when she heard the loud clap noise again, followed by another loud whine from one of the dogs. She had just made it to the end of the hallway when she was almost knocked down by Diamond, Queen's security dog, trying to push her back. Moving Diamond aside, she stepped into the dining room just as a large man pointed a gun at Bruno, one of the male Cane Corsos. Not wanting to see Bruno get hurt, she pointed the shotgun at the man and pulled the trigger.

Chapter 44

Queen was still trying to calm Key down when Key's phone rang again. They then pulled over and switched seats after the ordeal because Key found it difficult to concentrate or drive and was still sort of hyperventilating. She had stopped at the liquor store, grabbing a bottle of Patrón with two cups of ice and some pineapple juice. She had just finished making their cups, adding a slightly more alcohol to Key's cup than hers, when Key passed her the phone, saying, "Get this shit."

Queen instantly became irritated, hearing Twist's voice, until she heard Twist yelling Strip's name. Knowing she had just directed Strip and her mom to Bailey's room, she began wondering what could've been going on until she heard Strip asking someone where the fuck his lil' brother was. Knowing how overprotective Strip—and Memphis, for that matter—was over Pooh, she thought Twist was calling her in order to calm Strip down. But then she heard Pooh in the background.

"Why the fuck you call my brother? You think that's gon' save you, bitch ass niggas?"

Then she heard someone with a deep ass voice tell Pooh to put the gun down. Before she could fully grasp what was going on, she heard Strip say, "If my brother bust, I bust, so I advise you tell them lil' niggas to drop they shit."

She instantly got the message loud and clear. Strip, Twist, and whoever else were trying to talk Pooh down. Knowing they were only adding fuel to the fire, as she knew how it felt to have someone stand in your way when you wanted to prove a point, she screamed Twist's name and told her to put it on speakerphone.

Queen heard the go-ahead, but instead of talking to Pooh like everyone thought she was about to do, she said, "I don't know who the fuck this is, or why my lil' brother wanna splatter yo' shit, but if you and whoever the fuck else around you wanna walk out that bitch with y'all lives, I advise y'all lower y'all shit."

"Nawl, shorty, they in my crib, disrespecting my shit, and we got them surrounded. You tell them niggas to lower they shit, and you got my word, I'll let all of them leave the way they came!" Skitz said.

"Shit, I guess you niggas got a death wish then!" Queen said. "So I'ma say this and let the cards fall where the fuck they fall. Twist, you, Pooh, and Strip know what the fuck y'all signed up for and know we don't shelter no pussies around here, so if them niggas don't drop they shit in the next thirty seconds, y'all squeeze 'til it ain't nothing left in y'all joints. Y'all know what the fuck this is!"

Razor, being the oldest one, tried to intervene. "Hold on, Ms. Lady! Everybody got my word; won't nobody get hurt if everyone just lower they guns at the same time!"

Queen, not giving a fuck who the fuck dude was, said, "Fuck your word, nigga! I don't know you! Ten seconds done already passed! What's it gon' be?"

Skitz, seeing that he had a choice of whether to live or die, lowered his gun and told his youngsters to do the same. "Alright, we done lowered our shit. Now, what the fuck y'all want?" Skitz asked.

Queen answered, knowing the only way to calm Pooh all the way down, said, "Alright, baby boy, it's your party. What the deal is?"

"Shit, sis, I don't know!" Pooh said. "It's just somebody violated and gotta pay!"

"Is anyone there that's responsible for what happened or related to the motherfuckas that's responsible?" Queen asked.

Pooh shook his head like Queen could see him and said, "Nawl, but these niggas don't think shit stank either, sis!"

"Well, bro, we can't just go around punching niggas for shit they ain't did yet. They got the message though. I promise, if they violate, I'll take you back myself. Now, respect they shit, and tuck yo' tool so we can make examples out of the motherfuckas that's really responsible!" Queen said.

Pooh, knowing Queen was right, lowered his iron, thinking about what really could've just happened right then. He looked at Strip, Razor, and Twist before saying, "Let's go!"

Razor, trying to save face, looked at Skitz. "My bad, homie. This shit will never happen again."

Queen, hearing it, made sure she was heard. "I don't know who he was talking to, but I wouldn't count on it. Although y'all getting a pass today, I meant what I said. If anyone of you niggas get out of line, I'll be there right beside my brothers, busting my bitch, and won't nobody be able to stop me…"

Chapter 45

Stacy walked out of the bathroom, not sure of what the fuck happened or was going on. She saw Slim and Dee with their guns in their hands and her savior with his, looking like a deer caught in headlights. "What the fuck is you doing?" she asked her savior, looking at both Slim and Dee, telling them to lower their guns.

"Nawl, sis. Ya lil' boyfriend just got caught with his hand in the cookie jar!" Slim joked.

"First," Stacy said, getting heated. "This nigga ain't my boyfriend! Second, even if he was, it wouldn't be none of yo' fuckin' business, and third"—she turned toward her savior—"I asked you what the fuck are you doing, touching shit that don't belong to you nor concern you? And why the fuck do you got that gun out?"

Chauncey, still looking at the work, turned toward all of them. "Have y'all lost y'all fuckin' minds? We can't be sitting in here with all of this shit!"

Dee, not for all the talking, said, "Look, nigga. She already told you this shit don't concern you, so why the fuck are you tripping?"

Chauncey, still not believing his luck or what he was looking at and holding, said, "Nigga, is you crazy? Y'all left me in a room with over thirty million dollars in work sitting here! How the fuck don't it concern me?" He then turned toward Stacy. "You damn right I got my gun out and was prepared to shoot the first motherfucka that ran through that door!"

Dee busted out laughing. "Youngster, you buggin'. That ain't no fuckin' thirty million dollars' worth of work. Hell, we'll be lucky to get a million. And second, don't nobody know what we got in this bitch, so ain't nobody about to come through that door unless you called or told someone!"

Chauncey shook his head. "Nigga, I ain't called no fuckin' body. Hell, I don't even know where the fuck I am, and you right. This ain't no thirty million worth of work; it's way more!"

Slim and Dee both looked at each other before cracking up, laughing, tucking their guns, and looking at Stacy. "You know how to pick them, sis. Yo' boyfriend delusional as fuck!"

Stacy, glad the tension was easing, said, "I told you jack asses, he ain't my boyfriend!"

Slim, still laughing, said, "Well, at least tell us his name, sis."

Shaking her head, Stacy said, "Shit, I don't know!"

Slim and Dee, seeing she was serious, upped their guns again. "Well, who the fuck is he, and where did he come from?"

Shaking her head again, Stacy yelled, "Again, I don't fuckin' know! Stop asking me shit I don't know, and ask him!"

Chauncey, seeing shit was about to get real, lowered his gun and said, "Hold up. My name Chauncey, but y'all can call me Trouble C or TC for short, and I'm the only reason that she"— he pointed at Stacy—"still alive and still got all y'all work!"

Slim, not liking what he was hearing, walked over, still clutching his gun, and stepped in front of Stacy. "Explain!"

Chapter 46

Bailey was trying to finish stitching Toya up when Queen and Key knocked on the door. Not knowing who it was, she didn't say anything, hoping they would leave since she wasn't expecting anyone. She started getting worried, hearing the knocking continue. Hearing the knocking get louder, she was about to yell for them to go away when Toya beat her to the punch, yelling out, "Who the fuck is it!"

Not hearing anything, Bailey, thinking the worst since Pooh left, grabbed the .45 XD off the nightstand, only to be relieved to hear Queen's voice.

"Me, sugar!"

Jumping up and opening the door, Bailey was caught off guard and forced to take a step back when the door was forced open.

Shoving the door open, Queen burst into the room, staring at Bailey. "Why the fuck didn't you open the door or answer the first few times I knocked!"

Bailey, not wanting to admit that she was scared, just stood there until Toya said, "Pumpkin, leave that girl alone!"

Queen, already not liking Bailey, said, "Nawl, ma, why the fuck she just leave me standing outside, knocking—with everything going on!"

Bailey, knowing she had to save face, even if she got her ass beat, said, "That's exactly why I didn't answer. Bitch, with everything going on, I didn't know who the fuck it was!"

Before Queen could respond or slap the fuck out of Bailey like she wanted, both Toya and Key cracked up, laughing.

"Bitch, I know that's right. I wouldn't have either!" Key said.

Toya chimed in. "Yeah, I only did because I knew that .45 was on the dresser!"

Queen, thinking about it, laughed, shaking her head. "All y'all scary!"

Toya, seeing the cup her daughter was holding, yelled, "Hey, girl, what that is?"

Smiling, Queen said, "Patrón, suga. The bottle in the truck," before asking Key if she could grab it.

Key had just walked back into the room from grabbing the bottle when there was another knock on the door. Hearing it, everybody got quiet, looked at each other before cracking up, laughing, screaming, "Who is it!" at the same time.

Queen grabbed the .45 off the dresser that Bailey had set back down and was about to get up before she sighed in relief after hearing Pooh say, "Me!"

Before anyone could move, Bailey moved like lightning. She jumped up, snatched open the door, and threw her arms around Pooh.

Stepping into the room, Strip and Twist looked around at everybody who was still smiling or laughing, asking them what had been so funny. Before anyone could say anything, Bailey's phone rang…

Chapter 47

Bronze had been stressing all through the count because before locking down for shift change, he had sat at the phone for thirty-five minutes straight, calling everyone's numbers back-to-back-to-back with no answer. Thinking the worst, he was about to bang a nigga out, waiting for the phone that kept looking at him. He sucked his teeth when Twist finally answered the phone.

"Yo, what the fuck, lil' sis? What's going on?" Bronze snapped as soon as the operator said he could begin speaking.

"Shit, nigga, we been dealing with a lot out here!" Twist said, looking around at everyone.

"Is everything alright, and where the fuck is everybody?" Bronze asked.

"Yeah, for the most part," Twist said. "And everybody but big bro right here."

Bronze asked, "Who is everybody?"

Queen snatched the phone, taking it off speaker. "Nigga, she ain't about to do no fuckin' roll call. She said we all present. What's good?"

Bronze laughed, thinking Queen acted so much like Memphis that it was scary sometimes—even the way she always took charge like a boss every chance she got. Looking around, he said, "A lot, sis. I really need you and Twist to get down here to see me ASAP, as some things can't even be spoke out loud."

Queen, reading loud and clear, said, "Alright, I'll have Twist set up a visit for the first available spot in the morning. What else good?"

Bronze, not wanting to fake the fanfic, said, "Nothing, sis! Shit, to be honest, everything bad. I'll tell you everything at the visit. In the meantime, though, I need you to keep a leash and muzzle on everybody. Shit so hot right now; I saw on the news where they talking about bringing in the feds and the National Guard for all the murders happening around here!"

Queen, not liking anyone but Memphis checking her or telling her what to do, said, "Look, nigga. Anything that anybody did or had done needed to be done, and until everybody feel like our points been made, motherfuckas can cry all they want. But I will not tell anyone not to do anything that they feel like is best for The Circle, and that go for you too!"

Bronze, not being able to do or say anything, as she had a point, said, "On boss."

Queen was listening to Bronze tell her to bring him a new baby and at least eight hundred when she came to see him. Then Key handed her the phone, saying it was weird that a call came from Rosie's phone, but there was somebody named Jimmy on it.

Surprised, Queen handed Twist her phone back, telling her to tell Bronze she had him. Grabbing Key's phone, she lost her breath, hearing Jimmy tell her Rosie was in the hospital with him. Yeah, Rosie was okay, but she needed to get there like yesterday without anyone but security for her. There was no telling who was around.

Reading between the lines, she hung up after telling Jimmy she was on her way. Everybody was surprised when she looked at Twist. "Strap up. Let's ride," she said.

Chapter 48

Mandy was sitting in the bathroom, having second thoughts about what she was planning to do. Yes, she loved Blacc with everything she was made of, but she was a mother first and loved her children more. Plus, she couldn't understand how Blacc couldn't see he was being used and played by Mitch. Blacc had lived up to everything Mitch asked of him, yet Mitch hadn't done anything but promise Blacc more and more shit that he couldn't give unless Blacc gave it to him first.

That was something that Mandy tried to tell and show Blacc several times, but Blacc wouldn't listen or pay attention. The straw that broke the camel's back was when she heard someone ask Mitch how he had gotten out of the feds, and without shame or hesitation, Mitch—boldly and proudly, might she add—boasted about proffering on his old plug and competition. She told Blacc that, and she was told she'd heard wrong first before being completely ignored. Then she pulled it up on PACER to show him.

On top of that, she had been on Facebook earlier and knew all the stories about the killings going on were behind the shit that Mitch had been putting Blacc up to. Mandy, knowing how The Circle got down, knew it was only a matter of time before they found them hiding out in Mesa because, once again, Mitch had tricked Blacc into thinking that Mesa was far enough away from Phoenix for them to operate without The Circle finding out; which really was hilarious in itself, being that Blacc had been given the green light to operate out there by the local gangs and motorcycle clubs out that way because of his affiliation with The Circle. She knew it was only a matter of time before someone gave them up.

She was thinking all that to herself when Blacc stepped into the bathroom. He was drunker than she had ever seen him, telling her that he had fucked up and that she was right the whole time. Apparently, Blacc had finally questioned Mitch about what he had seen on PACER, and instead of Mitch denying it like Blacc thought and hoped he would, Mitch smiled and openly admitted it, even bragging about how he wished he had done it sooner. Blacc, knowing once a rat always a rat, knew if Mitch snitched on his people and childhood friends, then he would damn sure snitch on him, so he told Mandy he thought it best if she just took the kids and ran.

Hearing it, she nodded, only to get her heart broken when she asked him where she should go; he told her he didn't care, because it wasn't his problem anymore. Trying to hold her tears back, she asked him what she should do about money, only to be further crushed when he laughed and said that she had a pussy between her legs, so she should never go broke.

Knowing there was a big possibility they would kill her but spare the kids, she called Bailey, crying her eyes out, telling her everything.

Chapter 49

Razor doubled back to Skitz's house, not liking the way things ended because his name was on the line, and he would be damned if whoever the fuck old girl was made him look bad or put a blemish on his reputation. And that was what he told Twist, demanding to speak with Memphis immediately. What he wasn't expecting was for Twist to first deny, telling him who the fuck that was on the phone, or second to agree with whoever the fuck that was on the phone. Hell, even taking it a step further by saying they would have a problem if he didn't basically respect what the bitch on the phone had said and drop it.

Razor was amazed, seeing that he had been around Twist before she even understood her own sexuality, and he felt he was some sort of father figure to her. For her to back whoever that was to that extent meant old girl had to be someone very, very important, especially considering how both Pooh and Strip had bowed to her commands. He had to admit that even he was shocked by how whoever the fuck she was had bossed up over the phone, refusing to back down or fold, considering all odds were against them. He had no doubt she was indeed 100 percent serious with her ending threat.

He also knew how Skitz was and personally knew Skitz had to save face, too, or his own crew might see it as a sign of weakness and test his position or authority. Plus, Skitz was an OG with morals and still stood by his word. Sure, he had also heard some of the rumors Skitz had made about not liking how Memphis handled their ordeal, but he, like anyone else who had been in the game as long as they had, knew they were, in fact, only rumors.

Skitz knew he fucked up and made a major mistake by testing Memphis's gangster in front of everyone the way he had, so he had to accept the consequences of how Memphis reacted. His man's death was actually on Skitz himself, not Memphis, because had he not disrespected Memphis for no reason, his mans would still be alive. He knew and accepted that, but it was just hard to get the younger generation to understand. Although he tried telling them, it was like it had fallen on deaf ears. All the youngsters knew was trigger play: a life for a life.

That was another reason Razor found himself pulling back up in front of Skitz's house. He knew if he didn't fix things, they would only escalate, which was confirmed when Razor stepped out of the car.

The youngster Strip had upped his poles on stood up, upping his own, barking, "What the fuck you want, old timer?"

Razor, not used to being tried—twice now in one day—acted like he hadn't heard the youngster. He walked up the walkway. "Huh?"

The youngster made the mistake of looking around to make sure he had a crowd and an audience. The second the youngster's eyes left Razor's, Razor shot his arm out, punching the youngster in his throat. When the youngster dropped his gun, gasping for breath, he sat down where the youngster stood up from and told someone nearby to tell Skitz that Razor was outside and waiting to speak with him.

When Skitz stepped outside, seeing his nephew Cory on the ground and holding his throat, he couldn't do anything but laugh. Shaking his head, he told Razor to come in. "I been telling his lil' ass for years to watch how he talk to people, especially his elders."

Chapter 50

Jimmy had been pacing the hallway for about twenty minutes when he saw Queen and some other chick he had never seen before exit the elevator. Seeing her without Memphis was something he had never seen before, and for the first time, he realized how tall she actually was. He, himself, being six-feet-five, guessed that she had to be around six feet, maybe even six-one, which totally surprised the fuck out of him when he remembered that Memphis was only five-six, and that was on a good day. But anyone dealing with Memphis, especially over the phone, would swear he was a giant, and anyone who ever disrespected him and most definitely fought him would swear he was six-six. Somehow, his lil' azz would never back down, and somehow, he'd always win.

He laughed, thinking about how they always teased Memphis about having a Ceaser (or short-man) complex, as people had to watch how they joked with him, or they might get taken off on by him, with him thinking that they had tried him.

Jimmy, still upset by everything, didn't even give Queen a chance to speak before barking, "Where the fuck Memphis at!"

Twist, not knowing who the fuck Jimmy was, reached under her shirt, which wasn't lost on Jimmy or Queen, causing Jimmy to step up, smirking. "I wish you would."

Queen, knowing Jimmy was more like a brother to Memphis than his uncle, stopped Twist. "You don't wanna do that."

Before anyone could speak, Lil' Pooh ran around Jimmy, screaming, "Auntie Queen!" causing the tension to ease.

Queen bent down to pick the boy up, making both Jimmy and Twist take a step back, giving them extra space between the two.

Lil' Pooh, excited to see her and Twist, asked, "What's up, Twist?" Twist, used to Lil' Pooh always being around one of the guys, gave him a baby dap, but was surprised as fuck when he said, "Do y'all know my uncle?" pointing at Jimmy. Surprised by the fact, she involuntarily took another step back.

Smiling at Twist, Queen nodded, thankful for the respect she had just shown, as she tickled Lil' Pooh, saying, "Of course! I been knowing him way before you were thought about!"

Lil' Pooh, not liking that his news was old, looked at Queen, frowning. "Well, why am I just now getting to meet him?"

Queen, loving how the lil' boy always said exactly what he thought or what was on his mind—like all of the brothers—said, "That's something that you and him gotta talk about at a later time, okay? Now run and go make sure Nana okay."

Lil' Pooh, knowing that was one of his jobs that he took very seriously, kissed Queen's cheek and started to run off before stopping and putting his serious face on and looking at Jimmy. "Hey, Unc, we gon' finish that conversation later, okay?"

Jimmy, surprised by the seriousness he saw in the little boy's face, nodded and said, "Okay." Shaking his head, he turned back to Queen. "We gon' have to watch that lil' nigga."

Queen, being in total agreement, nodded. "Hell yeah, in more ways than one."

Jimmy exhaled, finally losing some of his tension, and opened his arms for a hug from Queen. "How you doing, niece?"

Queen slightly relaxed, hugging Jimmy. "Okay for the most part, Unc. It's just been a long ass, stressful day!"

Jimmy, not wanting it to be awkward as well as have a personal minute with Queen, turned to Twist with his hand out. "Twist, is it?"

Twist stepped forward, shaking his hand, and started to apologize.

Cutting her off, Jimmy said, "It's cool. I get it. You were just doing what you supposed to do, and by her bringing you, I'm sure you're good at what you do, so I need you to give me and Queen a minute. Rosie in the room with my mama, Lil' Pooh, and my sister. I need for you to make sure don't nobody outside of her medical care enter that room."

Twist nodded, relaxing, glad to get away from the weird, awkward situation.

Once Twist was out of hearing range, Jimmy turned back to Queen with a questioning look and said, "Now again, where is Memphis at?"

Chapter 51

Chauncey had just finished telling Slim, Dee, and Stacy his side of everything when Dee all of a sudden chuckled. "Repeat that shit, lil' nigga!"

Slim, amazed by it all, said, "Yeah, but let's eat while he doing it. That shit sounds like a movie or a book."

Stacy, glad to have something to do, grabbed the bag of food off the floor where Slim had dropped it, while Chauncey—or Trouble C, as he liked to be called—took them back through how he had been woken up by niggas trying to kick his door in, how he didn't have a chance to get dressed, only grabbing his shoes, his fire, and bullet proof vest, how he had run through the snow—basically naked—and fought off a pack of wild dogs, if she could believe that, which she did, as she had seen all the bite marks firsthand before the doctor had to sew them up, and he still made it to save her.

The part that really amazed her was how he still had the energy after all that to still fight with the guy that had attacked her, wrestling for the gun, even getting shot twice, killing the guy, getting her into the car, and getting them as far as he had before passing out.

She couldn't lie; hearing some of the story made her cringe on the inside, as having to relive her ordeal reminded her of how scared she had really been on the inside. When she was being attacked, she really thought that she was about to die. Her mind had closed up to that scene, so she didn't even realize that someone had called her several times until she felt Trouble C's hands taking the food and leading her to sit down.

That caused Slim and Dee to exchange glances. Slim, being closer to family than Dee, said, "Hold up, lil' nigga. You getting a lil' too fresh, ain't you?!"

Dee cracked up, laughing again, trying to ease the tension by saying, "Old ass nigga, don't nobody say or know what fresh is no more. Plus, as you can see, lil' sis ain't tripping. Now, back to this nigga Xavier. What's up with that nigga, youngsta?"

Chauncey, tired of feeling like these niggas were handling him, said, "Check it. First off, I done told you niggas what my name is, so y'all can kill all that youngster shit. Second, as y'all can see, shorty still in shock about everything that done happened, so if you niggas wanna finish this conversation or talk about all this work that y'all apparently sleep on, we can do that after we eat or in the room next door, especially since it smell like one of you niggas got some Zah on y'all."

Dee stood up, not being able to do anything but respect everything the lil' nigga had said. "Shit, nigga you got the food, so hand me a leg and a wing so we can grub." Slim laughed.

Chapter 52

Strip and Pooh couldn't believe what they were hearing come through Bailey's phone. Mandy had everyone in the room's undivided attention and mouths wide open, as nobody could deny the pain that was in her voice or how far Blacc had actually taken things while trying to get a position that, in honesty, was already his.

Strip and Pooh knew Memphis and Bronze had been trying to fall back for years, leaving Pooh and Blacc to run everything, as Strip had washed his hands of the dope game and only stayed as close to The Circle as he did to watch out for his two little brothers. On top of that, they had never heard of the nigga Mitch and couldn't understand—first, why the fuck he would come after them out of everyone, and second, why Blacc had betrayed his family in the first place for this nigga. Like, what was the connection?

Their thoughts were interrupted by Bailey telling Mandy to calm down, that she was gon' help her out of this situation. Hearing that, Pooh and Strip looked at each other, knowing if it was up to either of them, Mandy was about to die too, as she was just as guilty as Blacc; first, for not coming forward sooner or when she first learned of Blacc's treacherous thoughts, and secondly because if she would betray her children's father, the love of her life, they knew she would betray them if the squeeze was ever put on her. Third, and most importantly, because they knew Memphis seriously believed in that marriage shit. Because she and Blacc were married, they were one, so whatever one of them did, they both would be held responsible.

111

That was why Pooh cringed when Bailey gave Mandy her word on Lil' Pooh's life that she and her baby would not be hurt or harmed if she helped them line Blacc and Mitch up for them.

Mandy calmed slightly after hearing that, but she said she would only agree if she heard it from Memphis' mouth. She knew he had the final say in everything.

Pooh even grabbed the phone, trying to reassure her everything would be okay if she just told them where they were right then.

Crying again, Mandy apologized for everything but told them, "No!" It had to come from Memphis, as she knew his word was law. She explained this was her new number and to please pass it and her apologies to Memphis—even if it was just to spare her baby.

Chapter 53

Rosie was sitting in Ms. Whitney's hospital room, trying her best not to cry, as first, even though Ms. Whitney had not said a word or opened her eyes, it looked as if she was in so much pain; second, her head felt like it was about to split when, in actuality, it already had. She didn't know how powerful the shotgun was when she had pulled the trigger; the recoil had almost taken her shoulder off, causing the shotgun to hit her in the head, knocking her out. Third, in the ambulance, on the way to the hospital, she heard one of the medics talking about how the police had to shoot one of the dogs. She knew it had to be Bruno that attacked them when they kicked the door in after hearing the shotgun blast.

She was glad the other officer had only tased Diamond when he tried to check Rosie's pulse. She couldn't imagine how Queen would've taken Diamond's death. She was already worried about how Memphis was gonna react once he found out his dogs were dead; he treated the dogs like they were real kids instead of dogs.

Finally, she was worried about how much trouble she was gon' be in once her mom found out what she had done. Jimmy and the detectives told her she did the right thing, and she wasn't in any kind of trouble, especially because the shotgun was legally registered in her name, and the intruder had not only broken into her residence, but also shot and killed two of her dogs.

She just hoped Queen wasn't too mad at her for not staying in the house like she told her. She told the paramedics nurse she was okay and didn't need to go to the hospital, but they insisted. Plus, she wanted the police out of their house as quickly as possible because she knew her brother was gon' be madder about that than anything, which was why she was glad Jimmy called when he did.

Chapter 54

Twist had just finished booking Bronze's visit online and checking on Rosie and Ms. Rhonda when her phone rang. Seeing her home number flash across her screen, she smiled and answered, knowing it was her new little chocolate bunny she had left at her crib when she ran out to meet Razor. She was about to tell her to order something to eat if she was hungry and rush her off the phone when the girl—Shay—suddenly said, "I think it's somebody outside yo' crib trying to get in."

Twist, knowing with everything going on, there was a good possibility, still asked her why, as she still hadn't told the girl anything about herself.

The girl surprised the fuck out of her by saying, "Bitch, I'm from the hood. I know when somebody trying to break in, and I can tell by how you moved earlier that you ain't the type to call them people or want them in your shit, so quit fuckin' around and wasting time, and tell me where the fuck a pole at!"

Twist, instantly getting wet, got tongue-tied for a second before realizing someone could hurt her lil' bunny if she didn't open her mouth. She asked where she was in the house and couldn't help but laugh when the girl said, "In the bed where you left me, bitch!"

Shay laughed too, knowing what Twist was thinking, and promised she was still gon' be there waiting if Twist hurried the fuck up and told her where the pole was so she could handle this lil' business.

Twist told her in the top drawer of either nightstand, and she thought she fell in love when Shay said, "Shit, I'ma grab both bangers in case it's more than one, so hurry up, daddy, 'cause I'm about to get extra wet."

Twist would've left right then, had she driven her own shit and dealt with whatever fuckin' consequences either Memphis or Queen imposed later, but she had ridden with Queen in Key's truck. Queen was in a somewhat heated conversation with Jimmy. Shaking her head, laughing, she still couldn't believe that the big ass, white-looking nigga was Ms. Rhonda's son. Yeah, Ms. Rhonda was light-skinned, but everybody else had brown/black skin. *Maybe he's adopted or some shit,* she thought when her phone rang again.

Looking down at it, she saw Razor's name. Usually, she would've answered it without a second thought, but their last conversation made her hesitate. Yeah, she hated to talk to Razor the way she had, especially after all he had done for her. But no way was she about to go against The Circle—her family—for anybody, especially after hearing what Queen had said, as if it was the first time she got a glance at how down Queen was for the cause. She just didn't know if it was cap or not. Anyone could make threats or talk that tough shit over the phone. Only one, maybe two out of every ten, were actually about that life, and those odds were of motherfuckas straight out of the hood.

At the same time, Razor was family, too, so when he called back, she reluctantly answered, and for the second time in less than ten minutes, she was surprised…

Chapter 55

Queen had been steadily pushing ignore on the phone Bailey had given her while she spoke with Jimmy. For Jimmy not to be in the game, he said some valid things she needed to process and look into, because he was right: a lot of shit didn't add up or make sense.

For one, Memphis had never just upped and left the house in the middle of the night, especially without waking her up first. Hell, even if he was just about to let the dogs out to use the bathroom, he was either gon' tap her, asking if she wanted to hit the blunt, or try to put it to her lips in her sleep. Second, he couldn't go more than a couple of hours without calling her, and it was about to be twenty-four hours. Then, more fucked up things had happened in one day than in the last five to ten years they had been together.

On top of that, motherfuckas had to think he was all the way out of the picture for them to try all the fuck shit that they had. Plus, it had to be someone extremely close to know both the house address and mom's. Most importantly, though, they hadn't cared about the police presence, which meant they weren't gon' step until the job was done and finished, which also meant neither house was safe, especially now that them people had a chance to be inside both. She was totally in agreement with Jimmy selling both and finding new ones for them.

At the same time, she didn't like what he was saying about putting new motherfuckas in position to help them fade behind the scenes. She knew The Circle had put in major work to secure the spots and ground they had. Yeah, things had changed over the years, especially with the feds and DEA coming in, but she wanted to help Memphis build, not lose. Plus, she felt like all this was something that Memphis needed to do and decide, but she was definitely gon' bring all that up to Bronze in the morning when she saw him. She was wondering how her big daddy would handle or play all of this when she saw Twist coming out of the hospital room, speedwalking toward her.

Before she could tell Jimmy to give her a minute, Twist said, "Excuse me, Queen. I hate to interrupt, but it's a couple things that need your attention immediately. Plus, can I see the keys to Key's truck? I need to get to my house like yesterday."

Queen, seeing the concerned look on Twist's face, said, "Yeah, but I'm going with you!"

Chapter 56

Mandy had been waiting for Memphis to call her back and began to think she made a mistake by reaching out to them when there was a knock on the Penthouse suite they had been holed up in for the past couple of weeks. Tapping Blacc, she was disgusted that he was too drunk to understand her, let alone open the door.

She was relieved, thinking it was one of the maids coming to service the room when the door clicked open, but she saw Mitch sticking his head in the room. Seeing her, he asked her where Blacc was and stepped in, locking the door when she told him he was passed out, asleep. She had backed up to the bathroom area when Mitch suddenly grabbed her, squeezing her ass.

Trying to break away, she asked Mitch what the fuck he was doing when he suddenly slapped fire out of her ass. Pulling his gun out, he told her she had a choice: she could be by his side or outside, trying to fend for herself and her kids. Trying to do the honorable thing, she told him she would rather be outside than disrespect her vows and husband.

Shockingly, Mitch laughed at her, telling her the husband she once had was dead and gone, and the junkie lying in her bed would sell or pimp her out the first chance he got to keep from going dope sick. She began to cry, thinking of the words and shit Blacc had said to her earlier. Now, knowing how Mitch was controlling Blacc made her cry harder, which sadly only turned Mitch on more, she saw. Wrapping his hand around her throat, he snatched her panties to the side and was about to penetrate her when Blacc all of a sudden started calling for her. Hearing his drunken slur get louder and louder, Mitch knew it was only a matter of seconds before Blacc would get up to see where Mandy was.

Plus, he still needed Blacc to help get or set Strip up because, by now, Twist, Pooh, Queen, and Bronze should all be out of the picture, and the rest of their lil' ass circle couldn't function or run shit on their own. Knowing that, he told Mandy that he would kill her, the kids, and Blacc if she mentioned this, and her best bet was to really think about his offer. Everything was coming to a head soon, and he was about to be crowned the new king of Phoenix. He had just stepped back by the door when Blacc came around the corner.

Seeing Mitch, Blacc's face lit up, as he had begun Jonessing (fiening), until he noticed the gun in Mitch's hand and the tears coming down Mandy's face. Stepping in front of Mandy, he looked at Mitch. "What's with the gun, nigga?"

Mitch laughed to ease the tension. "Nigga, you know I keep this bitch on me. Plus, I was knocking on the door to give you back the key card you left on the table. But when I stepped in to put it down for you, your shorty bent the corner, scaring the shit out of me!"

Blacc looked back at Mandy, watching to see if she was going to say anything indicating differently or deny it, and he told Mitch, "Give him a minute," when she didn't say anything.

Mitch laughed, trying to play everything off. "Alright, my nigga. Hurry up tho'. You know what's up!"

Blacc turned back to Mandy when Mitch stepped out, asking, "What's up, baby? Talk to me."

Mandy, still terrified, didn't say anything but grabbed Blacc, asking him not to go.

Blacc, knowing how emotional Mandy was at times, thought this was one of her plays she used to always pull to keep him from going out with the guys. Laughing, he said,

"It's okay, babe. I'm not about to be gone long. Mitch just need my help with something real quick."

Mandy shook her head and went to pull away when Blacc suddenly noticed the bruise on her face.

Grabbing her chin, Blacc tried to remember what had happened before he passed out, but he couldn't recall anything, so he shamefully asked Mandy, "What happened?"

Crying harder, Mandy said, "Nothing! Just go!"

Hearing her words brought back many memories of when he used to hit her when they were younger. Kissing her face, Blacc said, "I'm sorry," before walking out to join Mitch.

Chapter 57

Xavier was madder than he had ever been in his entire fuckin' life. He really couldn't fuckin' understand for the life of him how his team had fucked up both plays even Ray Charles could've fuckin' seen.

First, he had been wining and dining the bitch Melissa for months before he got her to agree to set TC up. The fuckin' Ma'yote (nigga) was bad for business and in the fuckin' way. He was like a fuckin' money-making machine, getting money, not caring or respecting what the prices were. Any type of profit was a good profit for him, which was dumb in Xavier's eyes. Like, why sell a cow for thirty or forty fuckin' dollars when so many people were willing to pay eighty to a hundred dollars for it, especially if you were only paying fifteen to twenty dollars per cow? Hell, he even tried stepping to the dumb fuck, trying to agree on a set price of sixty dollars per cow—where they both would still see and make money—but the little bastard laughed in his face. He said no and that he was cool with what he was making!

His second cousin in Arizona, who married a fuckin' Ma'yote, out of every fuckin' thing, hooked him up with a Ma'yota named Memphis, who had tricked him by asking him how many cows his Rez could eat. When he responded with thousands, Memphis told him he would sell him cows for two dollars apiece and bring them to him if he agreed to buy at least a hundred thousand at a time. Not believing his ears, Xavier made a joke about bringing him a million, thinking Memphis was full of shit.

Two days later, his second cousin called to tell him she vouched for him with her life, and his cows would be arriving the next day. Not sure what to do or believe, he tried to call Memphis back to admit that he couldn't afford the whole million—at most, a quarter of that—but didn't get an answer. Sure, a lot of people in his tribe received twenty and thirty-thousand-dollar checks from the oil companies for drilling on their land, but coming up with two million dollars in cash overnight was impossible.

Then he remembered Melissa telling him about all the shoeboxes of money TC had in his closet. Sending his homies at TC had been easy since they didn't like the fact that a Ma'yote was living on their land, fuckin' one of their baddest bitches, and getting most of the money being passed around. They'd somehow missed him, but got away with almost three hundred thousand in cash, as well as about five thousand cows (blues). Sure, they killed the bitch Melissa, but hey, that was the price of business.

Xavier had just finished counting almost $1.2 million in cash after begging, borrowing, and pleading with everyone he could, trying to come up with the money, when the most beautiful thing in the world happened. The transporter—a female, at that—called, saying she was already on the Rez but lost. Thinking this was too good to be true, he sent three of his best men, telling them to make sure it wasn't a setup, and if it wasn't, if she was alone, snatch her ass up, but not to kill her until they were sure she had the work.

Everything went as planned, them circling to make sure she was alone, and Josh confirmed that Jax had, in fact, snatched her ass up, but Jax didn't show back up. Xavier, thinking Jax may have had his own bright ideas, sent Josh back up to the store, only to find out Jax was dead, and the car and girl were nowhere to be found.

Chapter 58

Shay had been lying in Twist's bed for a few hours, trying to decide when and what would be the best way to kill Twist. She had already looked all around the girl's house, finding the many guns the girl had hidden around, as well as the lil' money she had stashed. Although it was more money than she had ever seen at once, it wasn't enough to change her mind, as some shit was priceless.

She had to admit, though, she really was feeling the girl all the way around. The way she dressed, carried herself, and even put it down was different, as no one had ever made her cum back-to-back so many times in so many different ways. Hell, even the way Twist handled Mikey had had her panties dripping. She could actually see the fear in Mikey's face when she had seen her cousin kill plenty of niggas over the years without blinking twice. She wasn't sure, but she could almost swear that Mikey had pissed on himself, which, in itself, really made her wish she could be Twist's bitch or even be real with her, telling her what was up, but Mitch had her in a real jam.

Her mother and older sister, Melondy, had testified against Mitch, getting him thirty to life with a mandatory twenty-five years, yet somehow, he showed up on their doorstep a month ago, after only six years, demanding help to kill her sister's dad, Razor, or he would kill all of them. At first, they were just about to play along until he left and contacted Razor or their uncle, asking for their help until Mitch upped the score by taking her lil' sister, Kayla, saying he had already missed too much time with his daughter.

Hearing that and knowing what he did, everybody thought he was tripping until they saw the tears coming down their mother's face.

Razor's daughter, Carla, remembering how Mitch used to molest her and her older sister, begged Mitch not to take the little girl, even offering to go with him herself, but she only ended up getting knocked out.

Mitch promised not to bust her cherry and return her if they played along and helped, even promising them a hundred thousand, saying it would only take about four or five weeks. So far, they had only seen Kayla twice, the last time two days ago. The lil' girl was crying her eyes out and begging to come home.

Crying herself now, Shay was wiping her tears away when she first noticed the security lights come on, on the side of the house. Drying her face, she thought Twist had returned until the backyard light came on too. She knew she was in danger when she heard a window break downstairs. Calling Twist, really to see if she or their plan had been discovered, she slightly relaxed after hearing Twist basically cooing into the phone. So whoever was there had royally fucked up because no one was about to stop her from getting her little fuckin' sister back.

Chapter 59

Key and Toya were drunk as hell, laughing about the fucked-up ass day they'd had when Butch called Key's phone, yelling and talking crazy as fuck. Toya, hearing whoever yelling, snatched the phone, jokingly trying to calm whoever down, when Butch suddenly realized who was on the phone and got loud with her too. "Bitch, where my truck at, and why the fuck didn't nobody tell me Whitney was in the hospital!"

Toya, sobering up, screamed, "Fuck you and that truck, nigga! If you was a man and taking care of your business, wouldn't nobody have to tell yo' bitch ass anything!"

Strip, hearing her half of the conversation, became concerned, asking Toya who was on the phone. Instead of answering, she simply handed Strip the phone. Strip got on the phone and asked, "Who dis?" and almost busted a blood vessel when…

"Butch, nigga, and if you don't hurry up and bring me my truck, you gon' be laid in the hospital next to yo' mama!"

Strip exploded, saying, "Nigga, fuck yo' truck! And what the fuck you mean, my mama in the hospital?"

Everybody in the room looked at Pooh, thinking he had told Strip already, and dropped their heads, realizing Strip still didn't know.

Jumping up, Pooh snatched the phone from Strip, saying, "Come on, bro! I'll tell you everything on the way!"

Not backing down, Strip said, "Nawl, nigga, where the fuck my mama at, and what the fuck going on?"

Pooh, knowing what was about to happen, asked Butch where he was before hanging up after letting him know they were on their way. Taking a deep breath before standing up straight, he turned to Strip with tears in his eyes. "Mommy got hit, bro."

Before anyone could stop it or knew what was happening, Strip rushed Pooh, snatched him up, and slammed him against the wall, catching him with a two-piece—once in the gut, the other in the jaw—as he screamed, "What the fuck you mean, my mama got hit!"

Pooh, believing it was his fault since he was there, didn't even protest or fight back; he simply let the tears continue to run down his face.

Strip, seeing his brother's face, let him down, shaking his head. "Is she okay?"

Key, knowing more than anybody, spoke up. "She's alive, but in a coma."

Strip snapped again, yelling, "Well, who the fuck did it!"

Finally standing back up, Pooh snapped. "What the fuck you think I been doing all day, bro? I done literally hit up everybody that ever even looked at any of us wrong!"

Sighing loudly, Strip looked around before looking back at Pooh. "Well, why the fuck are we here instead of at the hospital, watching over her?"

Pooh shook his head. "That's a whole nother thing, bro. Now come on. I'll tell you everything on the way."

Before walking out, Pooh kissed Bailey, telling her he would be back, and Strip surprised everybody, including Toya and himself, when he bent over and kissed Toya slightly on the lips.

Chapter 60

Stacy really didn't have an appetite, but she ate a piece of chicken and some sides just so nobody would question her or look at her funny. Even though she didn't want to be alone, she did need a minute to herself, as today had been a long ass, excruciating day for her. Driving all night, just to get lost once she made it to her destination, had been frustrating as fuck, but being grabbed from behind was the scariest shit she had ever dealt with in her life.

She'd grown up with three brothers, an overprotective dad, and three more older boys pretending to be her brothers. Boys were afraid to even approach her, let alone touch her, and nobody ever disrespected her in any kind of way, so not only had she lost her bladder earlier, but hearing the tall, lanky dude say not to kill her yet made her heart literally stop.

Yes, she had been thankful for the compassion Trouble C had shown her, but he wasn't any of her brothers. Just seeing Dee and Slim had been a relief, but nothing could compare to the security her brothers brought. Running herself some bath water, she got up to close the door, but the fear of someone maybe coming through it stopped her.

Knowing the boys had gone next door to smoke and talk business, which could last hours, she stripped out of her soiled clothes and slowly lowered herself into the hot, steaming water, letting it relax all of the tension from her body. Closing her eyes, she wished that she had a blunt of her own to further help relax her, but she didn't dare ask Slim or Dee for any, knowing that neither would have given it to her in fear of her brothers or without at least checking with them first, and since she hadn't been able to get a hold of any of them, she knew it was a dead issue.

That was why she thought she was tripping when the strong smell of some Zah penetrated her nose. Opening her eyes, she saw Trouble C leaning against the door jam, blowing out smoke with a sexy smirk on his face. Not knowing what to do, she just looked at him, taking in his features, and she was totally caught off guard when he reached out the blunt to her, saying, "It looks like you can use this."

Taking it, she thought he was gon' say some lame line, but she was surprised again when he took his pole off his waist and set it on the toilet, saying, "We about to step out for a moment. It's off safety. If anyone besides one of us come through that door, you shoot first, and we'll deal with whatever later."

Walking out, Dee asked TC where the blunt he'd just rolled was and smirked when the youngster said he dropped it. He also saw that the bulge on the youngster's waist was gone. Nodding his head in approval, he told the youngster to be sure of what he was doing because shorty had more protection than the White House, and if he broke her heart, he'd be better off shooting himself than letting one of her brothers catch or find him.

Chapter 61

Skitz had just gotten done killing his main bitch, Ebony, putting her ass to sleep so he could slide out of the crib without answering a hundred questions tonight. He walked into the living room, finding his nephew Cory in there, smoking, playing the game, like he knew he would be.

"Hey, pause that shit, nephew. I need to holla at chu real quick," Skitz said.

Cory, in the zone, trying to level up, said, "Hold up, Unc. Let me smack this bitch like you just smacked Ebony thick ass!" without looking up, not knowing Skitz was in a zone of his own.

Then he heard the Glock 23 being cocked back and Skitz saying, "I ain't gon' ask you again. I'm just gon' dead that bitch!"

Cory looked up, seeing the seriousness on his uncle's face, and dropped the controller. "What's up, Unc?"

Skitz looked at his niece's son, whom he had taken in when he was nine to raise as his own. "In a couple hours, I got a meeting with them motherfuckas that came by the house earlier."

Cory, ready to get his lick back, said, "Hell yeah, let me go get my stick and ride with you, Unc."

Skitz laughed, knowing that, at sixteen, that was the same thing he would've said. "Nawl, nephew, it ain't that type of party. I done taught you how to gang bang. Now I'm about to show you how to get money. I'm about to link up with them to take us to the next level of the game."

Not seeing the bigger picture, Cory said, "Man, fuck that, Unc! They came by the hood today and disrespected the set. If anything, let's just rob them and do our own thing!"

Skitz shook his head, knowing that when he was younger, that was how he thought. "Then what, nephew? We get 'em for a few bricks or thousand and run through that; then what we gon' do?"

Cory dropped his head, knowing he had answered his uncle wrong. "So what's the plan?"

Skitz smiled, glad to see his nephew saw his error and said, "The plan is to tax them to teach us how they move, who their plug is, and the layout of the land so we can do our own thing."

Confused, Cory asked, "Wait, why would they pay us to teach us how to take over they shit?"

Laughing, Skitz said, "Because they weak and don't have no muscle of their own!"

Cory shook his head. "If you say so, Unc, but how do you know it's not a setup?"

Skitz stood up, laughing. "That's what I got you for. If anything happens, you know what to do…"

Chapter 62

Twist told Queen about setting the visit up with Bronze in the morning, as well as the meeting with Razor and Skitz at 2 a.m. at Denny's by the Casio.

Queen was low-key upset about Twist setting up a meeting with the opps, as far as she was concerned, but she was gon' run it by Pooh and Strip to see what they thought. Her mind was really on the news that Bailey had just told her about Mandy and Blacc. She still couldn't believe Blacc had switched up on his family like that. Hell, she and Bailey had been at the hospital in the delivery room when Mandy had their last child, their son, while Blacc and the boys had been out of town on a drill mission.

Shit, she and Memphis were the boy's Godparents and had bought his first everything, so she knew Memphis was gon' be both pissed but in total agreement with them sparing the kids' lives. Mandy was a different story, though, as she knew how her husband looked at marriage, so to him, Mandy was just as guilty as Blacc, and she knew one of Memphis's favorite lines was 'betrayal has no forgiveness and warrants death.' While she understood both Bailey and Pooh's plea for Mandy, as Bailey's stupid ass had put it on their child's life that she would be okay, she didn't know how she was gon' swing that or justify it to Memphis.

On top of that, she had no idea who the fuck this Mitch nigga was or why he wanted to die so badly. That was definitely what was about to happen, no matter if she had to lie to Mandy or not, because there was no way she was gon' try to explain to Memphis how she let Blacc or this fuck nigga Mitch slip through her fingers after all they had done when Mandy was basically begging her to line both of them up for them.

Then the shit with Butch was minor, compared to everything else that was going on, but just as important because, although none of the boys liked Butch and wouldn't lose any sleep if he was suddenly found somewhere slumped and full of bullet holes, he was still Stacy's father; and she loved her daddy almost as much if not more than her brothers, so she knew it would kill Stacy if something happened to him. That, in itself, would kill all of the boys, seeing their baby sister so torn up. She just didn't know how she was gon' get the point across to Strip while he was in the mood everyone told her he was.

Shit, she just remembered she hadn't even told the boys what happened with Stacy yet, nor had she called to check on all of them. Although Rosie told her she relayed her message to them, that was the last she heard. Once out of the meeting, she would call Key to get Slim's phone number since she knew the drill phone would've been left in AZ.

Then her mind drifted to how she was gon' tell Big Daddy that all of their babies except Diamond were gone. That nigga loved the dogs as if they were real fuckin' kids, even giving them allowances for treats and fuckin' dog toys and shit. And what were they going to do about their house now that it had been invaded, as she knew she would never feel totally safe there again, knowing that motherfuckas had actually gotten in and killed in there.

Her thoughts were interrupted by Twist tapping her. "Stay in the truck. I'm about to find out how niggas insides look on my wall."

Twist wasn't prepared for Queen's response when Queen opened her door and said, "On Larry, you must be smoking dope if you think I'm about to just sit in the truck while you have all the fun. Bitch, I want the first body!"

Chapter 63

Black was sitting in Mitch's bathroom, holding a tray with a nice pile of dog food on it. As bad as his body wanted him to snort a nice line of the powerful love drug, his mind couldn't get off the look on Mandy's face. It was a look he hadn't even come close to seeing in years. Back then, they were living fucked up, from motel to motel, him staying out all night, hustling just to make sure they had room money for the next day, enough for whatever food and hygiene shit that they may have needed, as well as re-up money to keep them afloat.

Back then, he used to get so fed up with her nagging him for small shit her homegirls and friends were having from fuckin' with local dope boys and robbers, and he sometimes used to slap her around just to get her to shut the fuck up. She didn't understand he was doing the best he could, especially without becoming a victim or getting locked up, as a lot of niggas his age were steadily falling victim to.

All that changed the day Memphis called his phone, fresh out of prison, asking him if he was hungry and telling him he wanted to talk to him about something. Black, thinking that Memphis was like most niggas fresh out of prison, looking to get a few dollars from people that they used to look out for, told Memphis he was busy and would get up with him in a few days. It wasn't that he didn't want to help his big homie; it was just bad timing, as he had just learned that Mandy was pregnant with their first child. Her mom, who couldn't see her precious baby girl pregnant—by a nigga, at that—had put her all the way out, so there was no more motel jumping, as the bigger Mandy got, the more she complained.

On top of that, motherfuckas had just popped up with some A-1, straight drop, making it hard for him to sell his work. Yeah, his rocks were bigger than theirs, but their quality was shitting on his, so he was having to take all the shorts, as well as stay out past most. He couldn't afford to break bread or take any breaks.

Memphis, being Memphis, had found out where he was staying at the time and was sitting in the motel room with Mandy, eating, when he came in for a quick break to check on her. He still remembered the proud look on Memphis's face, saying, "Baby boy about to be a father now. Congratulations." From that day forward, everything had changed.

Everything hadn't happened overnight, as there were still plenty of days they barely got by. But no more was it just him against the world. No, with Memphis came his brothers as well as support he, himself, couldn't believe at times. It was like, if one had it, they all had it, and if anybody needed anything, everybody would pitch in.

He also remembered the last time he put his hands on Mandy because it had been bad. So bad, in fact, that she had to be taken to the emergency room and was kept for several days. Black, being embarrassed as well as ashamed of what he did, called himself sliding to the next town over to get money, trying to get enough to finally get a place to call home.

He had gotten tired one night and thought he was about to close his eyes for a quick power nap. He had barely been asleep an hour when he felt a presence over him. Opening his eyes, he saw that he was surrounded by four masked men with guns aimed at him and someone else standing guard at the door. He was thinking it was a robbery or someone mad that he had been making money the last couple of days on their turf, so he attempted to hand it all over, when suddenly,

Memphis pulled off his ski mask, slapping it all out of his hands.

He looked up at Memphis with a confused look, and Memphis cocked his gun back, placing it to his head, telling him, "If it was anyone other than you that had hurt anyone in my family, they would be dead right now! That girl loves you and needs your help with that baby, which is the only reason I don't blow yo' motherfuckin' head off right now. But if you ever hurt her that way again, I'ma kill you myself and raise your baby as my own!"

Looking into Memphis's eyes, Black had no doubt that he meant every word he said, and it was further confirmed when Strip, Pooh, and Bronze all pulled their ski masks off, asking Memphis why he'd give him a chance if they already had him where he wouldn't be found.

He still remembered Memphis' words before he lowered his gun and walked out of the room. "Because he family!" Since then, he had never put his hands on Mandy again, so he knew he hadn't done it now...

Chapter 64

Lil' Pooh had been fighting to keep his eyes open for the last hour or so, but his little body had had it. Looking at his nana, he said, "Alright, Nana, it's time for me to get you in the bed!"

Ms. Rhonda looked down at Lil' Pooh and said, "What? You tired, sweetie?"

Lil' Pooh, feeling like he was being tested, poked his chest out and lied, saying, "No, but I know you are, and I don't want you to drop me!" causing both Jimmy and Rosie to crack up laughing at the little boy. Everyone had seen the lil' boy yawning.

Jimmy, trying to help his lil' nephew save face, said, "Nephew right. It's about time y'all all got some rest, as nobody will be able to help anyone if they sleep on they feet."

Rosie looked at Jimmy, saying, "Hey, you need some sleep too. You been up all day, and I been seeing you nod off too!"

Jimmy laughed. "Yeah, you right, but I'ma stay until Queen send somebody back up here to stay with Whitney. In the meantime, Rosie, me, and Queen in agreement that it ain't safe for none of y'all to return home yet, so I want you to look for some extended stay hotels or a big ass Airbnb."

Rosie's eyes lit up, glad to finally have something to do. "Okay, but whichever has to be pet-friendly, because Diamond still at the house, and we can't just leave her there, especially without the other dogs."

Jimmy dropped his head, knowing that, even being pet-friendly, most hotels would scram or flat-out refuse, seeing the damn-near two-hundred-pound Cane Corso. Not to mention, they didn't need any more trouble, and that was exactly what would happen with Diamond in a hotel setting. First of all, she really didn't like people, and second, not many men would stand a chance if Diamond's eyes fell on them. He wasn't sure if it was by accident or intention, but Diamond's hatred of men ran deep, which was why Memphis made her Queen's personal security guard. She even growled at Jimmy a couple of times in the past, low-key scaring the shit out of him.

Thinking about all that, along with everything that had happened in the past twenty-four hours, Jimmy said, "Yeah, Rosie, I think you'd better focus solely on the Airbnbs." Thinking about Diamond and everybody else who may have to stay there, he said, "The bigger, the better!"

Rosie, being modest, said, "Ummm, in what price range?"

Jimmy looked at his sister and said, "Price is not an issue. Just make sure whatever you find can accommodate everyone for at least a couple weeks."

Chapter 65

Shay was having second thoughts about being able to kill Twist. There wasn't fear or sucker shit like love, feelings, or emotions. Shit, she hadn't even known the bitch more than one day, and her sister came before all that shit anyway. No, it was the doubt of maybe underestimating the bitch, as whoever wanted the bitch dead had sent a small army to do it.

That was some Hollywood-type of shit, seeing that Twist wasn't Superman or Wonder Woman. Shit, the bitch was just one person, yet Shay counted three people she had killed already, and she knew there were still at least three or four motherfuckas in the house by then, steadily calling out each other's nicknames, which was hilarious. She just didn't know if she would be able to take all of them out by herself without being shot or killed in the crossfire.

At times like this, she wished she had her cousin Mikey by her side, as although she couldn't stand his tricking ways or loud, boastful habits, Mikey was a real gangster like her. He had been self-trained and battle-tested time after time, never letting her down. No, they weren't hitmen or professional killers like that, but being hungry or broke wasn't an option for either of them.

Playing Batman and Robin had turned into them playing Robinhood, robbing motherfuckas in the hood and surrounding cities, which more than a few times had ended up with them having to shoot their way out. They quickly found out the hard way, just because a motherfucka was sweet or a walking lick, that didn't mean his money didn't pay for real, certified killers, motherfuckas that didn't care if their boss was pussy, lived, or died. They were just in it for the money and body count.

Shit, she was thinking about the first time she had been shot when somebody yelled on ya right, blood. She had just turned when she saw a muzzle flash and was slammed back.

Chapter 66

Pooh had been telling Strip about everything that had taken place, including what Nana said when Strip told Pooh to make the second left, and Butch's job would be on the right. Instead of making the second left, Pooh pulled over, causing Strip to punch the dashboard in frustration.

"Damn, bro, I said the second left! What the fuck are you doing?" Strip snapped.

Pooh looked at his brother, knowing right now, he was a ticking time bomb. "Look, bro, I don't like the nigga Butch either, but he is our lil' sister's dad. So you can't kill him!"

Trying to play it off, Strip laughed and said, "I know that, nigga! The fuck are you talking about?"

Pooh shook his head, looking at his brother. "Bro, I know you and how you think, and even though you know we can get away with it, you know that shit gon' eat Stacy alive, and you know don't none of us ever wanna see her hurt!"

Seeing that he wasn't fooling his brother, Strip said, "Bro, look. All we gotta do is slump the nigga, throw a couple dollars around him to make it look like he bucked the jack, and baby Stacy for a few weeks!"

Pooh smirked, knowing Strip's plan would work. "Yeah, that would work, but who's to say baby sis gon' be alright after a few weeks? Plus, what about Mama? Yeah, she been cool away from the nigga this lil' time. But we both know she love the nigga, and most of the time, when she say she be out with her friends, she really be holed up in a hotel with the nigga."

Strip, not trying to hear any of that shit, said, "But what about all the times he used to hurt Mama? Most importantly, what about the shit he did to Memphis?"

Pooh shook his head, remembering the fright they all went through when Butch shot Memphis eight times, damn near killing him after Memphis fucked him up the last time Butch beat their mom. "Bro, I ain't about to keep making excuses for the nigga!" Pooh snapped. "Honestly, I want the nigga dead more than you! Shit, Memphis flatlined twice and was told that he would never walk again. But what did he do? Roll out the hospital three days later, looking for the nigga—"

"Shit, if the fuck nigga hadn't turned himself in and faced bro like a real man, we wouldn't be having this conversation right now, because he would be dead!" Strip said, cutting him off.

Pooh laughed. "You right, bro, but I was there, and what you don't know is that they gave the nigga Butch a hundred-thousand-dollar bond, and Memphis dropped twelve bands to pay it, saying he couldn't get to the nigga or his lick back if the nigga was locked up!"

Strip shook his head. "Hell nawl, bro, that ain't right, because the nigga never got out once he was locked up!"

Pooh laughed again. "I know, nigga. Again, I was there! I was the one sitting in front of the Maricopa jail, trying to talk bro out of the stupid shit he was trying. He had me pull right in front of the jail while he was holding an AR-15 with a drum on that bitch, waiting for the nigga Butch to walk out the front door."

Strip burst out laughing, imagining his brother doing some wild shit like that, and asked Pooh, "Well, what happened?"

Pooh said, "Shit, at first, we didn't know, but we later found out that the nigga Butch was getting processed out and got the bondman's information that showed him who had bonded him out, and when he saw Memphis's name on it, he knocked out the DO who had escorted him up to booking, yelling, 'Hell nawl! Y'all trying to line me up! Lock me the fuck back up!'"

Strip cracked up, laughing so hard that he literally had tears in his eyes. "Bro crazy as fuck," Strip managed to get out between laughter.

"Yeah, that nigga wild sometimes," Pooh said, agreeing with Strip

Strip said, "Fuck that. I still want the nigga tho'!"

Pooh said, "I tell you what, bro. Let's call Queen. If she say we can slump the nigga, I'll be the first one to squeeze!"

Strip shook his head, saying, "Come on, bro. You know Queen ain't gon' green light that!"

Pooh laughed. "You don't know sis as well as you think. Sis got a dark side that only me and Memphis really know about. She really low-key a witch that feed the dead!"

Strip cracked up, laughing. "Fuck that. She ain't gon' go against bro, tho'. Memphis spared the nigga because of lil' sis, so she ain't gon' go against his wishes, knowing he will fuck her up!"

Pooh shook his head. "Again, you ain't listening, bro. Queen fucked up. She'll okay us killing the nigga then gladly let Memphis fuck her up, knowing that he gon' baby and feed her after!"

Seeing Pooh was serious, Strip frowned his face up. "What type of weird, sick shit is that, bro?"

Pooh shook his head, shrugging. "I told you, bro. Queen fucked up! Her and bro got a weird ass relationship that don't nobody understand but them!"

Shaking his head, Strip said, "Fuck all that. I don't wanna get involved in none of that weird shit. Let's just get this nigga so we can finish all this shit and go check on Mama!"

Pooh laughed. "That's the first smart thing you done said all night!"

Chapter 67

TC had Slim and Dee honestly drooling all over themselves. In the room, they thought he told the biggest joke in the world when he said the little blue pills they could hardly sell for five dollars apiece back in Arizona went for as high as eighty to a hundred apiece out their way. They laughed and even mocked the youngster in the room, telling him he was dreaming, even going as far as telling him they would pay for his and Stacy's wedding if he could sell them for even twenty or thirty dollars apiece, knowing that neither would ever happen.

Now they weren't so sure, as the youngster had gone through almost a thousand of them at forty dollars a pop with motherfuckas not complaining but actually thanking him, even giving him free Zah and everything. Neither Slim nor Dee had ever seen anything like it and would swear they were dreaming if it wasn't for the bag of money sitting on the armrest between them. They literally were just sitting there, and every ten or fifteen minutes, the youngster would come and bring them knots and knots of money. They even acquired four or five new or damn-near new handguns and two AR's that they had in the trunk.

They honestly couldn't believe how sweet and lucrative this was and didn't understand what was going on when TC got in the back seat, messing with the seat, and told them to spin the block. Thinking the youngster just wanted to drop off more money and grab more work, maybe even blow one real quick, they laughed as Slim pulled off. Turning the corner on a side street, they were totally caught off guard when the youngster told them to stop right there. Slim, driving, didn't understand, as he didn't see a store or anything around, and there was a van right behind them. Then the youngster told Slim to slam on the fuckin' brakes.

Slim, thinking that the youngster was tripping, did it anyway and was totally blown away when the youngster hopped out, holding one of the AR's that had been in the trunk, chopping the van behind them the fuck up.

Hopping back in the car, Dee asked the youngster, "What the fuck!" and had no choice but to salute the youngster.

He said, "You old niggas slipping. That van bent the block twice and parked right across from y'all. I wasn't sure myself at first until it busted a bitch and got right behind us when we pulled off."

Slim said, "Well, what if it would have been the boys or them people?"

TC looked at him with a smirk, saying, "Shit, with everything we got in this bitch, it's a death sentence, and I'd rather them get it than us any day!"

Slim and Dee looked at each other, smiling. "My nigga!"

Dee stopped laughing. "Damn, this bitch was so lucrative," and was once again surprised when TC responded.

"Nawl, this wasn't shit. It's way more money in both North and South Dakota."

Chapter 68

Queen, true to her word, was the first one through the door when Twist unlocked it and shot a nigga in his face before Twist could close the door. Not waiting or wanting to be outdone in her own shit, Twist cleared both the living room and kitchen, killing another nigga, before catching a nigga twice in his back as he was trying to run out the back door.

Queen met her at the stairs leading to the second floor. "The other two rooms clear."

They both were surprised when a nigga upstairs yelled down that he was gon' kill this bitch if they didn't let him walk out.

Queen, not knowing or caring who the fuck was upstairs, with the day she had been having, screamed, "Man, fuck that bitch! If you kill her, you might as well kill yo'self because you dead anyway, nigga!"

Twist, not wanting her lil' chocolate bunny to get hurt or die, said, "Nigga, just send her down so we all can get the fuck out of here before them crackers get here!"

The nigga upstairs fucked up by saying, "Nawl, blood! Me and this bitch gon' walk out together!"

Queen, hearing his words, twisted up her mouth, gritting her teeth. "You might as well kill her anyway because you's a dead tampon," she said and started walking up the stairs, horrifying Twist.

Twist knew, if anything happened to Queen in her presence, she was gon' die anyway, so she ran up the stairs, jumping in front of Queen. At the top of the stairs, they saw nigga with a red bandanna tied around his face, holding a naked Shay in front of him with a revolver to her head.

Queen laughed at the nigga, looked at Shay, and said, "Look, nigga. Yeah, that bitch bad and all, but we still got at least ten apiece in our shit, while you maybe got eight at most, and that's only if it's a eight-shot, and you ain't busted any. Now, I don't give a fuck about that bitch, but I think my family might. So I'ma give you one chance to make it out of here alive before I shoot you and that bitch because I got too much other shit on my plate to be wasting time with this bullshit. Drop yo' gun and tell me who sent you in my people's shit, and you got my word I won't kill you."

The nigga, knowing he didn't have any other choice, dropped his gun and said, "Look, lady. The big homie sent us in here because Pooh came by earlier and shot our shit up for no reason. We didn't have no smoke with y'all, and I don't want none now."

Queen shook her head, believing the nigga, and lowered her gun. "Go ahead and get the fuck out of here."

Neither Queen nor Twist was prepared when they heard the shot, and blood spattered on them.

"Fuck dat! That bitch shot me!" Shay said.

Laughing, Queen said, "Yummy! She sexy and funny!"

Leaving, Twist had no doubts she had made the right choice earlier by going against Razor for Queen, and she honestly regretted agreeing to the meeting without first running it by Queen. She honestly just hoped Razor and Skitz were on the up and up because, if not, she vowed to kill both.

Chapter 69

Razor had been trying to get in touch with any of the boys after talking to Twist to get any kind of reassurance about Skitz's safety, and honestly, he regretted that he had put himself in their situation in the first place. If anything happened to Skitz, it was his ass on the line. On top of that, Skitz was his daughter's uncle and family, and he had been around Memphis and them long before they started calling themselves The Circle.

Yeah, he knew he really didn't have any say-so in anything they did, which had been proven when whoever the fuck was on the phone basically told him and everyone listening that his word wasn't shit. It was actually a low blow to his ego; at least with Memphis or Strip, they would take anything he said into consideration, respecting all the work he put in over the years.

That's it, he thought. Whoever had been on the phone had to be young because these youngsters didn't have any respect for their elders and felt like if you hadn't personally done anything for them, then you weren't their big homie, no matter if you paved the way for them or not.

He was thinking about all of this when his baby mama, Skitz's sister, called him, crying, telling him their old problem had returned. Razor, thinking maybe she was drunk or mistaken, laughed, telling her it was impossible. He quickly became serious, listening to her explain everything that happened, including her daughter agreeing to set up and kill Twist for him.

Chapter 7

Mitch thought about knocking on the bathroom door to make sure the nigga Blacc hadn't overdosed in there. At the same time, he didn't want to bother the nigga in case he was simply in a nod, as he honestly started to detest the nigga. The once fly, smooth, young nigga he used to pimp his slugs to before he went to prison was gone.

In his place was an arrogant ass nigga that spoke down to him when he first came home, like his Circle was the best thing in the world. Yeah, when he was in the feds, he heard of them, but from the stories he heard, they sounded more like a gang than an organization. They weren't trying to take over the city or anything, simply touching enough money to keep them above hood level.

To him, they had the power to take over the state; fuck just an area or city. On top of that, when he suggested to Blacc about meeting the nigga Memphis about buying some work, Blacc shut him down, saying Memphis didn't like meeting niggas, and that he, himself, could fill any order that he needed. Thinking that the youngster he used to serve twelve, sometimes thirteen, for the a hundred dollars was capping. He told him he wanted two bricks of Fetty and was surprised when Blacc responded that they could pick it up from his house after they got through partying.

He was thinking about simply robbing the nigga, but he heard, while they might not have been getting the most money in the city, they were one of the most feared and respected in the city. He knew he didn't have enough muscle to take them all on yet, so he spent forty of his last eighty thousand to buy the two bricks from Blacc, inquiring how he could get more if he wanted and, once again, was surprised when Blacc laughed and told him it was nothing, to just give him a number, and he could deliver.

Still sitting on a key of coke and heroin from before he left, he tried to make a couple of moves in the city but quickly found out that times had changed. Before he left, only big-time ballers and drug dealers could afford to go to the club, throwing five, ten, or even fifteen thousand dollars, attracting clientele to make the money back.

But now it seemed like everybody had money, even lames, and the fifteen thousand he had thrown wasn't even a big deal to the strippers. Knowing he couldn't afford to waste another fifteen G's, he tried fronting some work to a rap artist named DJ he met in the club that night, who'd also blown a bag and claimed to hang around all the superstars and celebrities, but he hadn't heard anything else from the nigga.

On top of that, word from back east was the niggas he used to compete with found out he was the one who put the feds on them, and he had money on his head. *I mean, shit, what was they thinking?* he thought. What did they think? That he was looking out for them or simply sending them clientele and money because they were friends? Shit no! Hell, where were they when his lawyer demanded more money? Where were they when the bitch and her daughter testified on him when he took them out of the projects and put a roof over their heads? Hell, he still couldn't believe the bitch had gone back to Razor over him.

The same thing went for his old plug. He couldn't believe the old Mexican had stopped taking his calls after he was sentenced, after all the money he had made for him. So what, he had an outstanding bill he hadn't paid? He felt he should've been given that and so much more for always being loyal to him, so he didn't feel bad about putting the DEA on him either. He just wished he could've known where the old man kept his stash.

That way, he wouldn't be constantly going through all the bullshit he was, trying to find out where Blacc, Memphis, or whoever the fuck Stash was. It was expensive ass fuck, bringing shooters from back east, as no one this way would fuck with The Circle. It wasn't hard to get Blacc turned out, seeing that he already liked playing with his nose. He simply started mixing dog food with the coke and let Blacc do the rest to himself. The task first came when Blacc started popping up with thousands, trying to cop with when nothing he could find could compete or even come close to the shit he still had from the old man.

On top of that, by then, Blacc became aware of what had taken place, but he also fucked up so much of Memphis's money that he had no choice but to go along with Mitch's plan. He just needed everything to fall into place and for Blacc to come through one more time by convincing Bronze to plug him in with their plug.

Chapter 71

Rosie found a huge ass cabin on the outskirts of Scottsdale. Being in a dominantly white neighborhood, it wasn't ideal for living purposes. It was going to be impossible to blend in or dodge nosy ass neighbors with 101 questions, like where they were from, what they did for work, or what brought them this way. But it was perfect as a vacation type of getaway, being that there were no niggas around that could possibly know motherfuckas who were where hunting or lurking for them.

On top of that, it hosted ten bedrooms, eight bathrooms, a full basement full of different games and activities, including a pool table, a swimming pool, and enough space in the back to keep Diamond curious for days. It was big enough to house everyone without feeling cooped up. Plus, what Jimmy really liked about it, besides the hunting rifles and shotguns it came with, was the high-tech security system, complete with motion detectors both inside and out. Googling it, he saw he would be able to both see and know if someone was coming to the cabin a full two or three minutes before they got there, both by the road or the trail that led to the house.

What he didn't like was the $1,400-a-night rate it was at or the $25,000 security deposit they required to secure it. Yeah, he had the money in his savings account and knew, either way, Memphis and the boys would replace it, but it was also a joint account with his wife, and the last thing he felt like doing was arguing with her regarding his family.

Coming from the suburbs—upper-middle class, at that—his wife had zero understanding of his family's way of life, and just like he thought, ten minutes after he handed Rosie his card and said to book it for two weeks, his wife called, screaming that they were being scammed or that somebody had hacked into their account. After getting her to calm down, telling her that it was he who made the transaction, she went from zero to two hundred in 6.3 seconds, wanting to know how the fuck he could spend almost $45,000 of their money without talking to her and, most importantly, why.

Not having the time, energy, or patience, he told her he didn't have time to talk about it, but he loved her and would call back later, before hanging up, not waiting for a response. What made him mad and got under his skin was when he turned around, his mom was shaking her head at him. Knowing he really didn't want to know the answer, he still asked, "What?" and was pissed off.

Ms. Rhonda laughed, saying, "Well, I still see who wears the pants and controls the bag in yo' marriage. What? You were too ashamed to tell yo' wife that you were finally helping your family for a change?"

Jimmy badly wanted to give her a piece of his mind or let her know it was just her that he couldn't stand, but he knew now wasn't the time or place to hear the screaming, denial, and fake tears she would instantly produce, as he had never met anyone her age who couldn't accept their fuck ups. Instead, he simply looked at his watch, knowing Queen called to say Butch would be arriving within thirty minutes to take over watch of Whitney.

Jimmy, knowing Butch loved Whitney just as much as anybody, knew Butch wouldn't let anything or anybody get to her without first going through him, which wouldn't be easy, seeing that Butch was an inch taller than him at six-five and 285 pounds of old iron muscle he had been wielding and carrying for damn near forty-plus years.

Chapter 72

Mandy had dozed off, but she felt her phone vibrating under her. Rolling over, she noticed she had missed three calls from an unknown, unfamiliar number. She texted the number back, asking who it was, but instead of a reply, the phone began ringing again. Saying *fuck it*, she answered, knowing only a few people knew her new number, and was surprised yet slightly happy to hear Queen's voice.

"What's up, girl?" she asked, in their usual, playful, white-girl banter.

Mandy let out a pent-up breath of relief that even Queen heard and felt over the phone.

"Damn, that bad, huh?" Queen said, trying to coax Mandy to talk, as they'd both been through this a few times together, dealing with their spouses.

Finally, Mandy spoke. "Yeah, sis, it's bad this time. It's really, really bad."

Queen, already knowing some of it from Bailey, said, "Yeah, it is, but I still need to hear and know what happened from you before we can try to find some type of solution."

Mandy got up, making sure the door was locked, even pushing a chair under the handle for extra security. "No disrespect, Queen, but is Memphis there? Because this is deeper than I think me and you can handle this time."

Queen tried and, already frustrated, said, "Nawl, bitch, he ain't available, and I really don't got time to baby or pacify yo' ass tonight. I still got a lot of shit I'm trying to get done, so if you ain't gon' talk for yourself, at least talk for yo' babies, as this yo' last chance to save them and maybe even you!"

Mandy, knowing Queen and hearing the truth in her words, said, "I ain't gon' lie to you, sis. He fucked up big this time."

Queen, already knowing this and then hearing her say it three times already, snapped. "Save the sis and drama shit, bitch, and just tell me everything you fuckin' know so I can try to save yo' dumb ass!"

With that, Mandy broke down, telling Queen everything, including Mitch trying to rape her.

Pulling up to the meeting, Queen said, "Mandy, I'm gon' ask you two more questions that's gon' determine both you and yo' babies future. First, where are y'all hiding out?"

Mandy, knowing either way, it was only a matter of time before they were found, said "Mesa, in the Sand Crest Hotel penthouse."

Second, Queen asked, "If I wanted you to give Mitch some pussy to get him in yo' room, would you?"

With tears in her eyes, Mandy said, "Anything for my babies…"

Queen shook her head, hating to hear the pain in what was once one of her sister's voice. "Keep yo' phone on you and this conversation to yourself. I'ma call you back shortly," she said, then hung up.

Chapter 73

Pooh was sitting sideways in the front passenger seat after picking Butch up, not for comfort or swag, but to keep a watchful eye on Strip, as the tension in the truck was so thick it could be bottled up and sold. He was thankful Queen called Butch and said whatever she had, as Pooh was unsure if his words or conversation with Strip had been enough.

What he did know was when they pulled up, Butch was hanging up from talking with Queen and looking at the truck weirdly. Pooh had been driving but got out to allow Butch to get in the driver's seat, and at first, Butch didn't move.

When Strip got out to get in the back seat, Butch tried joking with Strip. "Nawl, it's cool, bro. I'll jump in the back. I'm tired anyway."

Strip shook his head. "Nawl, nigga, you wanted yo' truck, so here you go," he said before getting in, slamming the back door.

Butch mumbled something and jumped in the driver's seat. "Man, one of you niggas, roll something up."

Pooh, seeing what was going on, pulled a wood out of his pocket. "Here, Strip. Twist this shit. You know you roll better than I do."

Strip shook his head, saying, "Nawl, I'm cool, bro."

That was an instant red flag; both Butch and Pooh knew that Strip smoked like a chimney.

Butch tried joking again, saying, "Man, why y'all done spoiled y'all sister like that? That girl be hitting my pockets like I don't work a regular nine-to-five!"

Strip, getting tired of all the jokes and fuckery, said, "Check it, nigga. I don't like or fuck with you, and the only reason I ain't slumped yo' ass yet is because of my mama and lil' sister."

Butch, knowing how Strip got down, said, "Damn, dude, I ain't never did shit to you. What's yo' problem with me?"

Strip, glad to finally be clearing the air, said, "Because of the shit you used to do to my mama and what you did to my brother."

Butch shook his head, knowing the youngster had a point, but glad to finally be able to voice his side. "Look, nigga, anything that happened between me and my wife was between me and my wife. Wait until you get married, and you'll understand, nigga. Y'all mama ain't the sweet, innocent angel y'all think she is. Not only do she lie for no reason, but she's also the biggest manipulator I ever met in my life!"

Strip, not wanting to hear it, said, "I don't give a fuck about none of that shit, nigga. You still shouldn't have put yo' hands on my mama, and what about my brother, fuck nigga?"

Butch, knowing he was playing with fire, said, "Yeah, I fucked up with both her and him! But nigga, how the fuck you think it felt to have my boy, a nigga I raised while you were off doing whatever the fuck, come home from prison and knock me the fuck out—in my house, in front of my wife and daughter—twice, as neither one of y'all know about the first fight we got into when he came home. Shit, I couldn't do nothing with the nigga on the hands tip, and the nigga wouldn't stop fuckin' with me after, knowing he got off on me!"

Pooh shook his head, trying to imagine how he would feel if Lil' Pooh ever did that kind of shit to him, and dropped his head, knowing he would've shot his ass too.

Butch kept on. "I love that boy. Matter of fact, I love all you niggas, which is why I turned myself in for what I had did. Nigga, I ain't scared of death. If it was anybody else, I would've kept at it until I got them, or they got me. Honestly, I couldn't cause y'all mama or sister that type of pain. Plus, me leaving y'all sister, my only child, them five years was the hardest thing I ever had to do."

Pooh looked in the back, but couldn't tell or judge Strip's facial expression by the darkness, but he could see that Butch had touched him by the fact that Strip didn't say anything after.

Pulling up at the hospital, Butch got out of the driver's seat and looked at Strip. "Give me a tool." Strip looked at the nigga like he lost his damn mind.

Butch said, "Nigga, I don't know what the fuck y'all done got into, but I'll die before I let anybody harm my wife in front of me, and y'all should know if I shot my own son, then I'ma smoke any nigga that pose me or her a threat."

Strip surprised the fuck out of Pooh when he looked at Butch and handed him two.

Chapter 74

TC asked Slim to stop at the smoke shop on the way back to the room. Pulling up to it, everybody couldn't help but laugh at seeing a dark-skinned nigga with dreads sitting on top of Stacy's car, bumping Kevin Gates while getting at a couple lil' hoes walking by.

Laughing, getting out of the back, TC said, "You niggas need anything out of here?"

Still laughing, Dee said, "Yeah, nigga, you know we all got the munchies, so just grab some shit."

Walking into the store, TC saw another nigga with a lot of gold on and dreads flashing the chick behind the cash register a knot of money, saying, "Come on, Joy. Fuck this job."

Laughing, TC grabbed some snacks and was grabbing some incense when the other nigga with dreads came in the store and tapped the nigga who had just been getting at the store clerk while nodding toward TC.

TC, peeping the play, pulled his pole out while pretending to still be browsing the incense. He looked over at both niggas staring at him and said, "Wrong choice, nigga. This ain't what y'all want."

Before either of the niggas with dreads could respond, the door opened with Dee stepping in with his hand under his shirt, looking at TC, saying, "You good, lil' bro?"

TC looked at the niggas with dreads with a smirk. "Are we?"

Both niggas looked at each other, smirking, and said, "Hell nawl, we trying to fuck with y'all."

With a mug on his face, TC said, "Explain."

The nigga that was flashing the money said, "My cousin just copped a couple of them thangz from y'all and called me, letting me know what they were going for, but before I made it over there, he called me back, saying you were gone."

TC smirked. "How y'all knew it's us they talking about?"

The other dread stepped forward. "What's the odds of two black Genesis with Arizona plates being here at the same time?"

Dee, not liking how they were singled out, said, "Shit, it looks like yo' car got Arizona plates too."

The dread with the jewelry on said, "Man, my smoker just rented me that car. If we couldn't find y'all, we was about to hit the road to go grab us some shit!"

Dee looked at him, smirking. "Rented?"

The nigga said, "Hell yeah. I gave him four blues for the week"

The chick behind the cash register said, "Hold up. You told me that was yo' auntie that's visiting car!"

The dread looked at her with a serious expression and said, "Shit, I would've told you it was my mama's car if you didn't already know that old ass Impala she got to get you to drive!" Dee and TC laughed at each other, smirking, knowing that if they had to, they both would've done the exact same thing. Then he said, "My name Jerry, but everybody call me J, and I ain't trying to tell y'all how to move, but y'all might wanna switch cars."

Dee was already thinking the same thing, but asked, "Why?"

J said, "Shit, with y'all prices, everybody in Des Moines looking for that bitch!"

Chapter 75

Bronze was hot and frustrated after tossing and turning most of the night. He lay in bed, wide awake, thinking about everything his lawyer said, as well as everything he needed to talk to Queen and Twist about in the morning. He was also concerned about why he hadn't heard from Memphis; they usually talked and joked around for a good hour or two every single day. He was praying it was because of him not having his baby anymore. Maybe Memphis just hadn't had a way to reach him.

Then again, he thought about the fact that nobody had heard from Memphis, something that also never happened. Memphis didn't have to be invited over; the nigga was like a party starter, just popping up at yo' house with a bottle or two, a big bag to blow, with forever on an EBT card, talking about barbequing or cooking. The nigga literally bought every food stamp he could find, sometimes just to give the kids in the neighborhood free rein in the store or, at the very least, ice cream or popsicles.

For the nigga to have no kids, he loved them with all his heart. He treated everyone he met like they were his own, so for him to be MIA for even an hour or two, let alone a whole fuckin' day, was frightening and mysterious as fuck, especially considering besides being a good nigga, he nigga also ran The Circle with an iron fist, always making sure that everybody was on top of their shit so that business ran smoothly, and that was exactly what had Bronze up, restless, thinking about right now.

Although he and his lawyer, Mr. Edwards, had a good rapport and friendship, they were not friends, and Mr. Edwards was a grinch when it came to his money. So, when he said he wanted $60,000, he actually wanted that and dinner because, somehow, you were going to always end up paying an extra forty or fifty dollars for this fee or that fee that he forgot to add on. Even if true, you would think it would be waived, considering how much money had been spent.

On top of that, the news of Ace not being paid was also surprising as fuck, seeing that Memphis had a thing about owing anybody anything, so he would have made sure Ace's money was put to the side way before he thought about spending a dollar. That, in itself, was also a huge headache and problem, being that they had to come up with Ace's money ASAP. He just wasn't sure of the ticket, as when he had called him, Ace didn't wanna say too much over the phone—jails, at that—and simply chit-chat about old times, and he made sure to let Bronze know he would be expecting a call tomorrow about his paper before hanging up.

On top of that stress, he knew bills still needed to be paid, as well as some of their workers in other gangs and organizations that supplied them with info that kept them as strong as they were. All this, bundled up, was a load he wasn't sure Queen would be able to tote and handle on her own, especially if motherfuckas knew both he and Memphis weren't on the scene. Yeah, with the help of the boys, he knew she would be able to keep their team in line. What he wasn't sure of was how long or, honestly, if Queen would have the guts to stomach some of the examples that sometimes had to be made.

Even though his lawyer said things were going well and progressing in his case, he knew it could still be a minute before he was back on the turf, given how dirty the crackers played.

Chapter 76

"Are you sure you're okay?" Twist asked Shay for the third time.

Shay nodded, saying, "Yeah. You don't have to keep coming out here, asking me that, or steadily bringing me drinks!"

Twist laughed before saying, "Ok," and walking back into Denny's. Seeing Queen sitting in the back on her phone made her wonder for the fifth or sixth time if this meeting was worth it or the right thing to do at this time, especially without Memphis present, as everyone knew he and Skitz still had unfinished business. But it was only on Skitz's side for real, as Memphis didn't care one way or the other. Hell, had it not been for Razor requesting it, she would have flat-out refused it. Being that Razor used his 'what have I really ever asked you for?' card, she agreed without hesitation or question. Queen, not knowing Razor, called Strip and Pooh, only agreeing to show and do it if the boys were there. They knew more about Skitz and Memphis's beef than she did, and didn't want to make any decisions without all the facts being on the table.

Adhering to Memphis's strict laws about knowing the surroundings, Queen had Twist get them there a full thirty minutes early, something she was starting to regret, as she felt like an open target, just sitting there. The good thing was, with everything going on, she used that time to check on everybody, as well as get a full update on everything that was happening, and it finally looked like things were making a huge turnaround in their favor, especially with what Slim and Dee had told her.

They definitely could use the money right now, with what Rosie told her Jimmy had spent, as she knew how Jimmy's wife was and couldn't imagine the type of situation it placed him in. The TC dude, she wasn't so sure about. Even Dee, of all people—which itself was weird, seeing that he didn't trust anybody—had vouched for him. Like Dee, she didn't trust people either and knew the nigga wasn't just helping them for no reason.

At the same time, she knew they kind of needed the lil' nigga. She just didn't know how long the lil' nigga would be breathing, seeing that Slim told her the lil' nigga was feeling Stacy and knew the boys were going to blow their tops when they heard about everything that was going on.

Her last thoughts were on the whole Blacc and Mitch shit. It was still hard for her to grasp that Blacc had not only switched sides, but he also helped a rat, snake motherfucka try to take all of them out. Knowing how Memphis thought, she knew he would have preferred Blacc to try to do or pull some shit like that for himself instead of for another nigga. That, in itself, was the definition of "EOP" (enemy of progress).

She knew he wouldn't be allowed to live, no matter what. She had just started to think about what to do about Mandy when the dude she presumed to be Razor walked in. Twist jumped to her feet, acknowledging him, even meeting him halfway to the table to dap him up and give him a brief hug.

Chapter 77

Blacc had been sitting on the toilet, staring at the dope, plotting for over an hour, when he heard Mitch in a deep and serious conversation with someone. Trying to be nosey and hear through the door, he became frustrated with not being able to pick everything up. What he did hear was Mitch yelling at someone to find Memphis, which was news and a frightening mystery to Blacc.

Mitch had convinced him that Memphis was already dead and gone. Knowing there was a chance Memphis was even still alive made Blacc pass gas, as not only did it change everything, but it also meant he was a dead man walking— shit, him, Mandy, and the kids. Memphis would put two and two together and know it wasn't a coincidence he called right before he was snatched up, or that he never sent whoever the nigga Ace was his bread. Because playing with his nose, he fucked up and thought he was going to be able to make the money back quickly by buying work for his old plug Mitch and getting that shit off in Mesa, where Memphis really didn't fuck around, especially since Mitch had that flame that even had him spending every dollar he had.

It wasn't until one night, after he had been out all day, trapping, he decided to do a bag himself to re-energize, that he realized the coke he had been snorting and selling was laced with boy, AKA dog food. He had woken up out of a nod, noticing that his pockets were empty, and all his jewelry was gone. Getting up, he saw his lookout dude was gone, and he had been robbed for everything.

Running back to Mitch, thinking he was going to help him out, he was shocked to find out that Mitch himself didn't have it like he first claimed to and even owed money for the bullshit ass coke he had gotten to stretch the dog food with. Knowing he was already fucked, he had come up with the bright idea of robbing Stacy, maybe even holding her for ransom by convincing Memphis to send Stacy instead of him on the road to North Dakota, saying that Stacy was a light-skinned chick driving by herself to a state full of colleges instead of his black ass, who the state troopers would fuck with just because of his skin in that cracker ass state. The plan was shot to shit when he called Memphis later that day, asking him which car or truck he wanted him to get ready for Stacy to take, and Memphis told him she was already gone, as it would be even less suspicious if she drove her own car.

Knowing there was probably no way to catch her, and having already asked Mitch for help with the robbery and kidnapping, he was left with the decision of either facing the music or setting Memphis up. He chose the latter, but he was told that Memphis bucked the jack and was killed, finding out now that Mitch lied had placed him and his family in deeper shit than he thought existed or was possible.

Chapter 78

Jimmy had just put his mom and Lil' Pooh in a Lyft to the Airbnb when Butch walked in. Giving Butch a minute alone with Whitney, Jimmy had Rosie order them a Lyft to the airport so they could get a rental car. Walking back into the room, Jimmy noticed that Butch was still in his work clothes and boots and asked if he was sure he could hold things down in his condition.

Butch gave Jimmy a look that made the hair on the back of his neck and arms rise, and said he was tired of motherfuckas questioning if he could protect his wife or not.

Jimmy shook his head, walking out, not wanting to get into a loud argument or debate in his sister's hospital room again. Plus, Jimmy didn't doubt that Butch could protect her; he just didn't want Butch falling asleep on the job after just getting off work.

Getting to the airport, Jimmy was both low-key spooked and confused when Rosie jumped on a shuttle bus, trying to get MIA on his ass.

Riding around in a circle at the airport, Rosie shook her head, knowing she had to go back and help. First, she knew her big brother, Memphis, would kick her ass if he found out that she had run from anything, definitely if she turned her back on family. Plus, she knew that there was no way Jimmy would be able to get Diamond in the car by himself without her trying to bite him or fuck him up. At the same time, no one had seen or heard from Memphis, which was scary as fuck to her—or the fact that Twist had fucked her head up in the hospital room when letting her know shit wasn't done or over.

Going to both Hertz and Enterprise, they were shocked to find out neither had cars, trucks, or SUVs. They both only had vans, with Enterprise having the full instead of a soccer-mom mini. Renting the full-size van, they stopped by the motel room, grabbing Toya, Key, and Bailey, knowing that everybody would be safer together than apart.

Leaving, Jimmy was joking about how it felt like they were about to go on a real vacation by driving the big ass van, when Rosie said, "Hey, I think that car is following us!"

Toya, knowing her daughter sometimes exaggerated, said, "Not tonight, Rosie. Mommy don't feel well."

Jimmy, knowing what Rosie had just gone through, ignored Toya's bitching. "Why, Rosie?"

Rosie responded by saying, "I'm a artist, and I remember the flames coming up the hood, as they look super cool!"

Jimmy looked in his sideview mirror and noticed the car had flames and looked slightly familiar. He just couldn't remember where from, so looking back at Rosie, he asked her, "Where did you first see it at?"

Rosie said, "At the Taco Bell, sitting across the street from their room!"

Jimmy still wasn't sure until the car started to speed up.

Bailey, seeing the lights get closer and brighter behind them, said, "Fuck! Do anybody got a gun on them?"

Everybody was looking around quietly and then was surprised when Rosie spoke up, saying, "Ummm, I do."

Chapter 79

Mandy had just finished packing her and her babies a small bag. After hanging up with Queen, she sat, thought, cried, and even screamed before deciding to help Queen first and then run for her life. There was no way she was going to leave her kids' livelihoods in another motherfuckas' hands. Fuck that. She would rather try her hardest to get her kids back to Clearwater, FL, with her family or die trying.

She just knew she had to at least help Queen kill Mitch. There was no way she was going to give him a chance to live after she felt like he had fucked up her and her family. Everything had been good before he came into their lives.

Her thoughts were interrupted by Blacc shouting, trying to get into the room. Remembering she'd left the chair behind the door, she jumped up and ran to it, not wanting to give away any idea of what she had planned. Moving the chair, she stepped back, bracing herself for either an argument or a slap. At this point, she wasn't sure what her husband would or would not do. What she did not see happening was him coming into the room with both a gun in his hand and tears in his eyes, saying that he was sorry, and she had to hurry up and pack because it was over.

Closing the door behind them, he went to the closet, grabbed a small bag, and said there was $60,000 in cash in the bag, and for her and the kids to take it and run. Sitting down beside Blacc, Mandy cried, begging him to come with them, but Blacc said he couldn't. He had to kill Mitch before Memphis and The Circle killed him.

Mandy, hearing this, began to cry harder. Seeing that, Blacc tried to calm her down, telling her it would be okay. Shaking her head with tears and snot running down her face, Mandy looked up, saying, "No! I fucked up!"

Blacc, not understanding, looked at her confusedly and was totally caught off guard when Mandy said, "I called Queen. She know everything, including where we are…"

Chapter 80

Pooh and Strip had just pulled up at Denny's when they saw a thick ass chick get out of the back of Key's truck, holding her shoulder. They laughed, watching her ass jiggle as she walked into the restaurant while they finished their blunt, thinking about what they would and could do to the chick, given the chance, even going as far as making a lil' side bet of who would fuck first.

Pooh stopped laughing for a minute, looking at Strip and asked him, "What was up with that shit at the room?"

Strip acted dumb at first, trying to play it off, until he saw Pooh wasn't letting it go. "Alright, bro. Look, mama kinda sexy to me and way more gangsta than you think!"

Pooh looked at him, laughing, saying, "Yeah, but that's Queen mama, nigga!"

Shrugging, Strip said, "Nigga, I don't give a fuck. I ain't trying to marry her. I'm just saying she sexy to me, and I wouldn't mind fuckin' on that."

Pooh laughed, thinking his brother was crazy as hell, but seeing that he was dead ass serious. "Hold on, bro—"

Cutting him off, Strip said, "I wouldn't even be here or alive if it wasn't for shorty!"

Pooh, putting that into perspective, simply said, "Dammnn. Alright!" leaving it at that, knowing no matter what he, Queen, or Memphis said, Strip was going to try to flip Toya.

Seeing Queen text him, Strip said, "Come on. Let's take care of this lil' shit and see what these niggas talking about."

Walking into the restaurant, they saw Queen, Twist, and Razor sitting at a table, having a strategic conversation, with Razor trying to convince Queen of something and Twist just sitting, looking as if he was stuck in neutral or something.

Twist exhaled in relief, seeing the boys enter, and excused herself to give them room, as well as check on her lil' chocolate bunny, as from the looks of things, they were about to be there for a minute, especially seeing that Skitz hadn't even arrived yet. Knowing that, she smiled, thinking about the way Shay's ass jiggled when she walked by.

Chapter 81

Meeting Jerry, or "J" as he liked to be called, and his cousin Dread turned out to be a blessing in disguise. Not only was J a natural-born hustler with the gift of gab, being able to sell anything, but he was also an all-around street nigga who grew up with and around J's—or junkies—so he knew how to not only spot them but also relate to them. That made them happy to spend their money with him.

Dread, on the other hand, was funny as fuck, but also a certified street nigga who really just liked to drill shit, sometimes for no reason at all. That made him and J two niggas not to be fucked with in their small city of Des Moines.

On top of that, Slim thought linking up with them would give them the green light to lock the city down. Trouble C had other plans, though, as he honestly wanted to get back to North Dakota as soon as possible. Without knowing it, he was thinking like a boss when he made a deal with Jerry and Dread: only supply them in Des Moines at the low price of ten dollars apiece if they bought a boat (a thousand) or more at a time.

Jerry quickly agreed to it, even starting off with three boats. Dee, seeing how easy it had been for them to run through the thousand they had that day, knew Memphis would agree to how he was thinking, fronted them another three boats at fifteen dollars a piece. Even if they never saw or heard from the lil' niggas again, the $30,000 they just spent more than paid for the six thousand pills they gave them.

But if the lil' niggas did honor their word, there was no limit to how much money could be made. Sweetening the deal, Slim agreed to bring the work to them if they bought at least ten boats at a time or met them halfway if five or more were bought. Either way, Jerry couldn't complain, as he was looking at more work than he had ever had or even seen at once, and couldn't even imagine how much he was about to touch. Looking at his cousin Dread, he swore to him that they would never go broke or hungry again.

Dee, making sure they had multiple numbers to reach them, told them they were now part of The Circle. Dread laughed, saying, "Hell yeah," not knowing what he had just agreed to.

Pulling off, Slim dropped Dee and TC off at the small airport to rent a car after all agreed it was time to get the fuck out of dodge. Pulling up to the room, Slim shook his head, thinking things couldn't have been more right. Their room door was open, and Stacy's room door burst open to reveal a guy holding his lower back and trying to run. Stacy was coming out the door with a sheet wrapped around her, holding the gun firmly and squeezing the trigger twice…

Chapter 82

Instead of riding with Razor or allowing his nephew to ride with him like he asked, Skitz decided to go alone to show he didn't fear anyone and could handle his own business. Plus, this *really* was business to him and a move he definitely wanted to make, not just for himself, but for the whole set, as this would really move them up a few levels, as well as give them a stronger hold on the city than they had now. Even though they had Cali on lock, Arizona was right next door, and it had been going toward the other way for years now.

Walking through the door, Skitz saw Razor, Pooh, Strip, and a woman with purple and blue locks sitting at a table in the back. Looking around, he saw no one else had brought any bodyguards or shooters, so he knew he had made the right choice by coming alone. Nearing the table, he saw everyone look his way and, for a second, wondered if he would ever be able to fully trust them. Knowing they probably felt the same way, he slightly relaxed when Razor stood up, grabbing another chair from a different table so he could sit.

Sitting down, he saw the woman with the locs lowkey sizing him up. Looking at Razor, he said, "No disrespect to all that's present, but I would've felt more comfortable with this arrangement if Memphis himself had showed up so we could've put all the bullshit and rumors to rest and behind us."

Pooh went to speak when the woman raised her hand, cutting him off. "I am my husband. My presence alone should show you that he takes this arrangement serious. Unfortunately, he had other business matters already made when Razor called, requesting this one. Now, since I've already become acquainted with Razor, let me tell you who I am and where I stand on all this, seeing how Razor has vouched and went to bat for you. My name is Queen, and I simply have one question for you. How the fuck are we to trust you after my husband killed ya mans, as well as shot you?"

Skitz, thankful to have his Glock on his waist, as well as a baby 9 in his back pocket, said, "Easy. I know I violated first, so I have no choice but to live with the consequences, just as I'm sure he knows he would if he ever crossed that line."

Strip stood up. "Wait. Is that a threat, nigga?"

Skitz said, "Nawl, it's a fact! Shit, if we to do mutual business, respect got to go both ways. I promise my homies gon' squeeze at any OPP or motherfucka you want murked, but in return, I gotta know that y'all ain't gon' be sending us on no dummy missions or low-key trying to lil-boy us. I don't doubt that the money gon' always be on point. My biggest concern is that y'all gon' treat us as business partners and not just pawns!"

Queen nodded her head, understanding what he was saying, and was about to agree to the terms when Razor suddenly jumped up, aiming his gun behind Queen.

Skitz looked up, seeing his niece standing in front of Twist, holding her shoulder with blood all over her shirt, and stood up, aiming his gun at Queen, causing Pooh and Strip to jump up, aiming their guns at Skitz.

Chapter 83

Shay was mad as fuck that Twist had stopped eating her pussy right before she came, claiming she had to get back to the meeting. Shay, not giving a fuck about their meeting, didn't want Twist touching her right then, so she marched out of the bathroom, snatching away from Twist each time she tried to stop or touch her, not giving a fuck until she saw her uncle sitting at the table with the chick she had met at Twist's house, named Queen.

Thinking it was some sort of setup, she turned around, swinging on Twist, before turning around and noticing the nigga Razor had a gun aimed at her. She froze up, seeing her uncle jump up and aim a gun at Queen. The two niggas that were sitting next to Queen jumped up, aiming bangers at her uncle.

She opened her mouth to scream when Twist suddenly pushed her behind her, aiming her tool at Razor. Skitz, hearing his niece scream while falling, turned his gun on Razor, preparing to squeeze, thinking that Razor had shot his niece. Then he was shot multiple times by Pooh and Strip. Razor, seeing this, aimed his gun at Shay, about to squeeze, when Twist popped his melon, shooting him back-to-back in the face.

Queen just shook her head, sitting there, not understanding what the fuck just happened or how shit had turned sour so quickly.

Chapter 84

Toya was speechless and couldn't wrap her mind around what her youngest daughter Rosie had just said until Jimmy said, "Oh, shit! They're trying to come up on the side of us!"

Hearing this, Bailey reached up front, yelling, "Let me see that bitch!"

Rosie lifted her jacket, handing Bailey the pole she had been carrying on her waist that Twist had given her at the hospital. She tried to ignore the look on her mom's face, knowing that a long, long discussion was coming. She was just hoping Queen or Memphis would be there to save her. For some reason, her mom still acted like she was a baby or something.

All those thoughts went out the window when Bailey opened the side door, shooting a few shots into the passenger window, causing the car to swerve, then dramatically slow down.

They thought it was over until Jimmy said, "Fuck! Here they come again, on the right side now!"

Bailey tried handing the gun to Key to get their pursuers off them, but Key flat-out refused, saying, "Hell no! I ain't no damn Charlie's Angel!"

Rosie, already knowing she was in trouble, said, "Girl, let me see that!" She lowered her window, aimed at the driver, and pulled the trigger several times, causing the car to swerve and then flip. Putting the gun back on her waist, she looked back, seeing her mom's mouth wide open, and asked Jimmy for her phone back so she could call Queen to make sure she was going to meet them or, hopefully, beat them to the Airbnb.

Chapter 85

Mitch was fuckin' the shit out of a lil' Piasa bitch he could barely understand. All he knew was he had seen the sexy, young bitch eating a gas station sandwich on the side of the store like she hadn't eaten in days. Knowing Mesa was an easy entry point into the country from Mexico, Mitch took a chance and flashed the bitch a knot of money with his arms open like 'what's up?'

The bitch looked at him and the knot of money, blushed, and jumped in the car without saying a word. Hell, he didn't even know she couldn't speak English until he was nine inches inside of her, trying to get her to quiet down, and all the bitch kept saying was, 'No Ingles!'

He had just busted one of the biggest nuts in his life when Blacc came out of the bathroom, moving faster than he usually did after getting high. Stopping Blacc, he reminded him they were in this together, and within the next day or two, he was going to have to pull himself together enough to convince Bronze to plug him in with the plug. Blacc, knowing it would never happen if Memphis were still alive, easily agreed with Mitch, trying to hurry back to Mandy.

Mitch, sensing something wasn't right, told Blacc to sit down for a minute.

Blacc sat down, watching Mitch usher the chick he had been fucking into the bathroom, wondering how the fuck he allowed this nigga to trick his life off like he did.

Seeing the look on Blacc's face, Mitch smirked. "What's up?"

Frowning, Blacc couldn't help asking him what the fuck really happened in the room between him and Mandy.

Laughing, Mitch acted dumb at first, asking, "What do you mean?" before shrugging. "Mandy came on to me, bro. She even told me that she would leave you for me if I promised to take care of her and the kids! I couldn't do you like that, though, so I pushed her off me, causing my gun to fall."

Knowing Mandy, Blacc immediately knew that was a lie and was about to confront Mitch about it when Mitch's phone rang. Knowing he couldn't kill Mitch without first making sure Mandy and the kids were straight, he crept out of the room while Mitch was on the phone.

Mitch hung the phone up, hating this fake ass mob family more than anything. He couldn't understand how it was so hard to kill just four motherfuckas. He had just found out that two more of his on-loan-but-hired shooters were dead. On top of that, he had no more work left, nor any place to get any. Now that word had spread around the East Coast that he was hot, nobody wanted to fuck with him, no matter how much money he tried throwing around.

Checking on the lil' bitch, Mitch was walking out of the bathroom when he saw that Blacc had split on him, which also gave him pause, seeing that Blacc had become a liability now and could finger him for all types of shit. Thinking about splitting and running himself, he lifted the mattress, looking at every dollar he had, knowing $300,000 without a plug or a way to flip it wasn't shit when on the run.

A lot of motherfuckas didn't understand that running from the law or anybody was expensive as fuck these days, especially if you were by yourself and didn't have help. That was why he lowkey really needed Mandy and the kids, as they could've been his perfect cover story. Thinking about Mandy, he thought about what he had just told Blacc, and ran out of the room, hoping he wasn't too late.

Chapter 86

Stacy had been lying in the bed, dozing, when she heard the door crack open. Thinking it was Trouble C trying not to wake her, she turned over, about to tell him she was still up, when she saw a dude in all black standing over the table with all the work sitting on it. He was whispering to another guy.

Remembering what TC said about someone killing all of them for that type of work, Stacy reached over, grabbed the gun TC had left her, aimed, and shot the first guy in his back before moving on to the next dude just as he dove to the floor. Standing up, she reached to turn on the lamp and was punched in the face. Falling back, she felt her shirt being ripped off.

Scared they could overpower her, she jumped back, hitting her head against the wall. Squeezing the trigger, she shot the guy once in his chest and twice in the head. Hearing a door slam, she turned, seeing that the door to the connecting room had been closed. Grabbing a sheet to cover herself, she ran to the door, snatching it open just in time to see the dude she had shot coming out the other door. Seeing him look back, she aimed and shot him twice in the back, although she really had been aiming for his head. She was about to panic, feeling blood run down her face, until she saw Slim parking.

Slim knew they only had a few minutes before the police would arrive, and he knew there was no way they would be able to talk their way out of this shit with that much work in the room, even if they were in the right. So, he told Stacy to hurry up and get dressed while he packed the car up.

He had just finished putting everything from both rooms in the car when the motel manager came out, asking what had happened. Slim was about to tell him he didn't know until he saw how the manager was staring at the car, thinking he was trying to memorize it for the cops. Slim drew his gun and was about to shoot the nosey motherfucka until the dude said, "Oh shit! It's-it's y'all! Man, if you just give me a couple of them thangz, I'll go erase the cameras, as well as clear the two room logs!"

Smirking, Slim said, "What?"

The motel manager ran around to the back of the car, looked at the tags, and said, "I know what's up! Fuck with me, and I'll make it appear that y'all was never even here!"

Laughing, Slim said, "Hurry up and do it, and I'll give you more than just a few!"

Chapter 87

Blacc didn't want to believe what Mandy just said, but the pain in her sobs and tears on her face told him it was true. Thinking about it, he really couldn't blame her, as he also knew if she had to choose between him and the kids, it was always going to be the kids, something he was honestly proud of her for. He had helped raise her, watching her grow from a spoiled teenager into the sexy, beautiful woman she was.

Laughing, he had a flashback to how scared she was when they first found out they were about to be parents. Whether she remembered or not, he had made her promise back then that no matter what, they would always put their baby before themselves, and knowing how The Circle got down, he was proud that she had kept her word.

Mandy had begun to cry harder, thinking his laughter was toward her fuck up, until Blacc began to kiss her on her neck, telling her it was okay.

Pulling her robe open, Blacc started sucking on her collarbone, making his way down to her firm, juicy titties. Lifting her bra straight over them, he began sucking on one nipple before having his way with both. It was amazing to him to realize for the first time that, even after all these years, her titties were as firm and perky as when he first met her. The only difference was that they had gotten bigger, and she had gotten them pierced.

Hearing her moan pushed him further into his trance of how shy she was the first time they made love. Playing with her belly button ring while easing her back, he lifted her

183

petite waist while pulling her panties down at the same time. Smelling her pussy juices, he lifted her knees while slightly pushing them back. Looking at her pretty, pink, shaved pussy, he had to admit it was still the fattest and prettiest pussy he had ever seen in his life. Parting her fat pussy lips, he swore her clit was sitting up like a juicy ass grape, waiting to be eaten.

Taking her clit between his lips, he began sucking and lightly tugging on it while gripping both of her ass cheeks, squeezing and massaging them as if she were riding his dick. By this time, Mandy was moaning so loudly that he was sure the kids would bust in on them at any second. He felt her tense up, and Mandy began begging him to stop and put his dick in. Ignoring her, he held her down and began sucking on her clit harder, causing her to scream and hump his face hard as if she was taking the dick like a big girl.

Convulsing, her body literally started jumping like she had been electrocuted or something. She screamed while flooding his mouth and face with the sweetest fruit smoothie he had ever tasted. After letting his head go, she attempted to sit up to return the favor. He firmly and roughly pushed her back down, kissed his way back up, bit down on her bottom lip, and shoved his dick all the way inside of her, causing her to both scream and wrap her legs around his back.

Wrapping his arms around her hands, he pinned them behind her head, causing her to slightly arch her back, allowing him to dig further into her stomach than he ever had before. As he went deeper and deeper with each stroke, neither noticed that Mitch had entered their room or the hatred for both he had plastered across his face. Hearing Mandy scream as she came again, Mitch punched the wall in frustration as he stalked back out of the room.

Blacc, on the other hand, became more aroused, causing Mandy to lose her breath as she felt him swell inside of her more. Blacc, sensing it had become more pain than pleasure for Mandy, let her legs down and slowly rolled her over, giving her room to breathe, as well as allowing her to control how much dick she took.

Mandy, sensing that their time was coming to an end, stopped Blacc, looked into his eyes, and said, "I don't care how much it hurts. I want you to give me another piece of you." Blacc looked at her, unsure of what she meant, so Mandy got on all fours and said, "Nigga, I don't care if you split my insides. Put a baby in me so, even if I die tomorrow, at least I'd go with you inside of me."

Seeing the tears in her eyes but the serious, determined look on her face, Blacc rammed his dick into her, trying his best to touch every wall and inch of her insides until they both came, crying out together on the bed. They lay together in bliss and peace for the first time in years.

Their mood was ruined when Mandy's phone rang, and she saw it was Queen. Blacc felt Mandy tense up and automatically knew who was calling. Standing up, he kissed her on the forehead with tears in his eyes, placed the bag of money that had fallen back on the bed, and said, "Do whatever she ask or tell you," before getting dressed and walking out of the room.

Chapter 88

Pooh and Strip looked around the restaurant before looking at each other, not wanting to, but knowing what they had to do, so they both took off running, rounding up the waiters and cooks before telling Queen, Twist, and whoever the other bitch was to get the fuck out of there. They knew that, even if Denny's didn't have cameras, there were too many witnesses to simply threaten.

Placing all six workers in a booth, Strip stood watch over them while Pooh ran around, pouring as much cooking oil and grease over everything he could. When Pooh was done, Strip asked the team leader where the camera controls were. Seeing it, Strip ejected both discs before shutting down the system. Walking back to the booth, the team lead tried to run, causing Strip to shoot her in the back of the head.

Pooh, hearing a shot, thought it was a signal and shot the other five workers. Strip, seeing it was a done deal, lit a menu and dropped it in a spill of grease, causing a chain reaction, which led to the entire restaurant going up in flames.

Chapter 89

At the Airbnb, Queen had just finished reassuring Rosie that she was there, when Strip and Pooh walked in. Seeing the gloomy looks on their faces, she grabbed a bottle off the bar with shot glasses, bringing it back to the table and pouring each of them shots. Pooh went to speak when Queen suddenly cut him off, saying, "What's done is done. We didn't ask for none of that shit. Nor can we take back what the fuck happened. The best thing any one of us can do is thank God that we still alive, as well as pray for forgiveness for the shit that we all have had to do tonight."

Strip poured himself another shot and raised it. "To the end of a fucked up day!"

Before he could drink up, Queen stopped him. "We got one more problem to deal with tonight."

Pooh looked at Queen, thinking about the five innocent people he had just killed, and asked Queen, "Could it wait?"

When Queen told them what Rosie had just called and told her, the boys looked at each other, saying, "Blacc?" which was confirmed when Queen nodded.

Strip, already fed up with the day, slammed his shot glass down that was still full. "Fuck it. Let's get this shit over with!"

Twist, hearing the glass slam, came running into the room, asking what was going on. Pooh telling her they still had to deal with the Blacc and Mitch shit tonight caused Twist to sigh, throw back the shot Strip had just set down, and say, "Let me go get ready."

Strip, on the other side, asked, "So what's the move?" causing Queen to pick up the phone and call Mandy's number.

Chapter 90

Trouble C was still laughing, clowning Dee for how the fat, country bumpkin had tried to all-the-way-out holler at Dee at the rental car place, even going as far as telling him what all she would do to him if he was simply there to pick her up when she got off in an hour.

Dee himself couldn't help laughing, knowing that he wouldn't ever admit it, but if it was late night, and he couldn't find anything else to slam or flip, he would definitely slam and take her big ass down before he went dry dick or to sleep with no pussy. To Dee, all big girls weren't off-limits to him, as there were some that were both cute and sexy as a motherfucka.

Them hoes were just big as hell. During the cold, it was cool, but in Arizona, where the temperatures could still be as high as seventy or eighty degrees at night, that shit wasn't happening. He didn't like his own sweat and damn sure wouldn't be laid up with any fat bitch snoring and sweating all over him.

Plus, only Memphis knew about the time he had gotten into it with the fat bitch Monica, and she sat on him, not letting him go anywhere for two to three hours straight. She got off him, almost cracking one of his ribs, when Memphis had popped up at his house to check on him. Hell, he was so mad and embarrassed that day that he would've killed Monica if Memphis hadn't stopped him and taken the gun from him.

To make matters worse, after they finished smoking a blunt, laughing about the shit, they walked back in the house, out the backyard, to find the fat bitch still there in the kitchen, eating pizza and fries, crying, and asking Dee why he didn't love her anymore. It took Dee threatening Memphis to tell about the night he almost got tricked to get him to shut up about it and not tell anybody. Since then, he hadn't brought a big bitch back to his house, simply hitting them at their shit or in motels.

But after the day they had, he was low-key thinking about doubling back and slaying the big bitch just to say he fucked and got some pussy—in Iowa, of all places. Plus, the way the big girl had been talking was low-key a turn on, as he really wanted to see if she could do everything she promised.

All those thoughts died when they saw the motel they had been checked into was yellow-taped off with police cars everywhere. Riding past, they were thinking about hitting the E-Way and getting ghost when they saw a police cruiser blocking the on-ramp. They were riding around, honestly just bending corners, until TC noticed Slim walking out of a twenty-four-hour Walgreens.

Chapter 91

Mitch was honestly hot and low-key jealous, walking back to his own room. He couldn't believe the bitch Mandy had not only turned him down, but still fucked the nigga Blacc as if her life depended on it after telling her the nigga was a junkie now.

Opening his room door, he saw the sexy lil' Piasa bitch painting her toenails while watching Telemundo. Seeing her wiggling to the music coming off the Spanish TV show instantly brought him out of his funk and gave him a hard-on out of this world. As he walked toward the bed, she licked her lips, looking at him, and without him saying one thing, she crawled to the edge of the bed, getting on all fours when he unbuckled his belt and dropped his pants.

Spreading her pussy lips, he rammed his dick in her while grabbing her long, pretty hair, trying to make her scream as loud as Mandy had been screaming. Pushing her head into the bed, making her ass arch more, he couldn't help visualizing her being Mandy, and he knew she belonged to him, watching cum coat his dick as he continued drilling her ass.

Pulling out, he skeeted all over her back and ass and thought he was done until she quickly rolled over, grabbing his dick, sucking it, and getting it back right. Taking his dick and playing with her pussy with it, she pulled him closer while lifting her legs straight into the air, still holding his dick, sliding it back into her tight, little pussy.

Feeling her cum on his dick again sent him over the edge, causing him to bust before he could pull all the way out of her. Laughing, she fell on the bed with his dick still jumping, shooting nut all over her stomach and breasts, and he thought he could spend forever with her when she went to playing in it, putting it in her mouth.

Hearing someone knock on the door, she jumped up and ran to it before looking back at him, holding her arms out. Grabbing his gun, he nodded, and she opened the door, looking like a fucking goddess. Blacc saw her and was about to turn his head until she giggled, turned, and ran back to jump into the bed beside Mitch. Walking in, Blacc saw Mitch putting his gun down, smiling.

"This the life," he said.

Chapter 92

Jimmy and the girls had just pulled into the Airbnb when Strip, Pooh, and Twist were walking out. Bailey tried to stop Pooh, but Pooh simply kissed her and told her to get a room ready, and he would be back shortly. Toya grabbed Strip's hand as he passed and asked if he was okay.

Strip, seeing her tipsy—a shot or two away from being drunk—responded, "Yeah," and asked how she was.

Toya, overhearing what Pooh had told Bailey, smirked and asked him, "Should she get a room ready too?"

Strip, really tired and not in the mood, especially for no drunk pussy, said, "Nawl, you good. Maybe another time."

Toya, not used to being denied or turned down, snatched her hand away, asking Strip what the fuck his problem was.

Strip, not in the mood for an argument either, simply shook his head and walked away.

Key, seeing the whole exchange, tried talking to Toya to calm her down, but Toya snatched away from her too, storming into the house, hoping there was at least a bottle or two, as everyone had her fucked up.

Chapter 93

Shay was sitting in the room, wondering how the fuck she was going to warn Mitch. After ear hustling, when Twist walked out to check out the loud noise, she heard Queen talking to someone about setting up Blacc and Mitch. Knowing it wasn't a coincidence, she begged Twist not to leave her or to let her go with her, but Twist denied both. In all honesty, she really didn't give a fuck about Mitch, but she couldn't allow them to kill him without first finding out where the fuck her little sister was.

She already felt sick to her stomach, watching the fuck niggas Strip and Pooh kill her uncle, and vowed that she was going to make them pay. Getting up, she walked into the dining room, seeing Queen still sitting at the table, now staring at her.

Trying to feel Queen out, she said, "Hey, um, do you know when Twist will be back?"

Queen shook her head. "No. Plus, the last time I checked, Twist was grown."

Switching tactics, she looked at Queen and said, "Well, do you have something we can smoke or blow on?" Once again, she was disappointed.

"No, but if Twist call, I'll tell her to pick something up for you."

Sucking her teeth, Shay said, "Well, shit, can I at least use your phone?"

Queen said, "Look. I don't know you, I don't trust you, and I really ain't feeling all these questions you asking me at three o'clock in the fuckin' morning. Now, I know it's been a long day and night for you, and I can understand if you still a lil' jumpy, so it's a bottle sitting right there. If you feel like you need something, take that motherfucka and drink as much as you want, and I advise calling it a night. If not, I'm sure Twist picked a room with a TV in it. Even if you want to rent a movie or something, that's cool. Either way, you're Twist's guest, and as you see and know, she ain't here. So just do us all a favor and slide back into y'all room until she gets back."

Toya was walking by when Shay asked, "Well, what if I don't wanna stay until she gets back?"

Queen stood up. "Look, bitch. I done told yo' ass already what it is. I don't know what you and Twist got going on; neither do I give a fuck. What I do know is, I got too much on my fuckin' mind to keep answering all them sucker ass questions you keep asking me."

Toya said, "Hold up, Pumpkin. You can't make that girl stay here if she don't wanna."

Queen looked at her mom, more pissed off, and said, "Look, Suga. It's after three o'clock in the fuckin' morning. In da morning. If she wanna leave, I'll have Lyft, Uber, or whoever the fuck she wanna call or use to take her wherever the fuck she wanna go. But as of now, she need to get the fuck out of my face, as my patience real, real thin right now!"

Hearing the commotion, Jimmy came in. "What's the fuckin' problem now?"

Shay, seeing a man, tried playing on his emotions. "I don't know y'all, and I just wanna go home!"

Confused, Jimmy looked at Queen. "What's up, niece? Why can't she go home if she wants to?"

Frowning, Queen looked at Jimmy. "I gave my answer. You wasn't here, and I ain't repeating my fuckin' self!"

Shay, seeing there was no win, said, "Well, can I at least use one of y'all phones so I can at least call or text my mom to let her know I'm okay?"

Before Queen could respond, Toya handed Shay her phone. "Here, baby!"

Chapter 94

Mandy had both of her babies dressed and was waiting for Strip or Pooh to call so she could buzz them up. Queen promised her that if she helped them get both Blacc and Mitch, she would spare the babies and even her for the night, and they would talk about her situation tomorrow. Knowing that was the best she could ask for right now, she easily agreed.

She had just finished feeding her infant when Strip called to tell her they were downstairs. Calling downstairs, she told the desk to send them up, and less than two minutes later, she was opening the door for them.

Pooh stepped in first, shaking his head at her as he passed. Seeing that Pooh had spent so much time with her and Blacc, she couldn't help but drop her head, silently crying.

Strip, not for all the emotional shit, said, "Hey, save them tears for Queen. All I wanna know is where yo' punk ass husband and his rat ass friend at."

Drying her eyes, she told Strip Mitch's room number and asked him what else he wanted her to do. Strip looked at her, wishing he could say die, then shoot her in the face, seeing all the hurt, pain, and shit her husband and his friend had caused.

Pooh, guessing what his brother was thinking, shook his head at him before looking at Mandy. "Call and get him up here! But make sure you keep it on speakerphone, and don't try no slick shit."

Chapter 95

Leaving the motel, Slim and Stacy were about to hit the E-Way until Slim looked over and saw blood dripping off Stacy's chin. Remembering the twenty-four-hour pharmacy he saw by the Popeye's earlier, Slim headed straight there, not knowing where the blood was coming from, as he couldn't get Stacy to say anything. Running in, Slim bought everything from gauze to liquid stitches.

Cleaning her face up, Slim saw that besides a knot on the back of her head, she only had a black eye and a small tear where some of her stitches had come loose. Filling the tear with liquid stitch (super glue), he went back into the store, getting her some Ibuprofen and something to drink.

Coming out, he saw a silver Jeep Wagoner speeding up and upped on it, about to squeeze, when he saw Dee behind the wheel. TC jumped out before the truck fully stopped, running around to Stacy's side. Seeing her eye and bloody shirt, TC upped his pole, running up on Slim, asking him what the fuck had happened. Dee, seeing this, jumped between them before telling TC to put his gun up unless he was going to shoot both of them.

Even though Dee liked the youngster, Slim was like his brother, and he would shoot the fuck out of the youngster before he ever allowed him to shoot or even hurt Slim. At the same time, Dee wanted to know what had happened, too, as he was more worried about how Memphis, Strip, and Pooh were going to take it than how TC felt.

Before Slim could answer, Stacy said, "It wasn't his fault! Hell, he wasn't even there!"

Slim walked around Dee and TC, handing Stacy the Ibuprofen and water. "Niggas ran in the room before I made it back. Somehow, lil' sis got a gun and smoked both of them."

Hearing that, Dee looked at TC, grateful the lil' nigga did what he had.

Seeing the police ride by, Slim said, "Man, we got to find a way to get out this small ass town or find somewhere to lay low until the morning. I don't want to try to even rent another room around this bitch."

Dee looked at him. "I may have somewhere."

Everyone looked at TC when he cracked up, laughing hard as fuck.

Chapter 96

Blacc was laughing, hearing the Piasa chick, Maria, tell him about her adventure from Chihuahua, Mexico, to Mesa, Arizona, USA, simply because of her overprotective, drug-dealing brother, Gomez. Mitch was getting mad, steadily asking Blacc what she was saying and what was so funny, being that he didn't understand Spanish.

Once again, Blacc found himself both grateful for Memphis and feeling regret. He remembered how Memphis used to make him sit down while the Spanish chick, Camila, he was fucking taught him, Strip, Pooh, and Blacc how to speak both Spanish and Portuguese. He was listening to her tell him how her brother had his own little poppy field, when Mandy called his phone, telling him she needed to see him for a quick second.

Blacc, knowing what was up and what time it was, excused himself from Maria and Mitch, stood up, stepped aside, and whispered to Mandy that he loved her and was sorry it had to end this way, but to please make sure his kids knew he loved them. Seeing Mitch looking at him, he told her to come downstairs and get the money for the food order, hoping whoever was listening would catch the message.

He was hanging up the phone when Mitch's phone suddenly rang. Mitch looked at the phone confusedly and hit ignore, only for whoever to call right back.

Blacc was laughing while at the same time telling Maria to get ready to drop to the floor and cover her head. Maria laughed, thinking he was playing, and asked what he meant, when Mitch suddenly stood up, answering his phone.

Chapter 97

Slim was trying his best to hold his laughter in, watching Dee walk out of the rental car place, holding the big chick's hand. TC, on the other hand, was in the back seat, dying from laughter, causing Stacy to become upset. Stacy had been big once before, and she knew how it felt to be laughed at or picked on.

Turning around in the seat, Stacy told TC, "If you knew what was good for you, you would shut the fuck up!" causing Slim to crack up laughing when TC instantly stopped laughing, sat up, and apologized to Stacy.

Stacy thought it was sweet, watching Dee open the truck door for the cute, chubby girl before turning on the truck and running over to them.

Approaching Slim's window, Dee told them that the girl's name was Kierra, and she lived alone on the outskirts of town in a small two-bedroom house with a garage, and to follow them. He went to walk away before stopping, mumbling, "Oh yeah, we about to stop for breakfast."

TC, forever a clown, smirked. "What, bro? I couldn't hear you," he said while trying not to laugh.

Slim, hearing TC while seeing the look on Dee's face as he walked away, cracking up, caused TC to laugh uncontrollably. Stacy shook her head and told them both to shut the fuck up.

Chapter 98

Mitch had been trying his best not to let his true feelings show, as once again, the nigga Blacc had him feeling some type of way. For the life of him, he didn't understand how, as black as the nigga Blacc was, the nigga spoke and understood fluent Spanish like he was Mexican or some shit.

On top of that, he had been peeping the lil' flirtatious looks the lil' bitch had been giving Blacc and already had it set in his head that he was going to beat her ass as soon as Blacc left. There was no way he was going to let her disrespect him or let the nigga Blacc know he was getting under his skin. Fuck no. To him, he was too much of a player and a boss to ever let a junkie outdo him or one-up him.

Mitch noticed Blacc hadn't been acting like the fiend he had become though. Usually, by now, Mitch would've told Blacc several times to slow down on the dog food, yet so far, Blacc hadn't even asked him for any. On top of that, Mitch caught Blacc looking at his phone several times, when usually, Blacc didn't care if he had that bitch on him or not, which was why Mitch was so glued in when it rang. Blacc whispered into it, which was normal, seeing as Mandy stayed in and on his ass.

What stood out to Mitch was Blacc telling Mandy to come get the money for her food. First, who the fuck was delivering at four in the morning? Second, Mitch knew Mandy would never leave her kids in the room alone, even if just to get the money for some food. So, A: Who the fuck else was in the room with her? Or B: Who the fuck was Blacc telling to come to his room?

His thoughts came to a stop when he saw an unfamiliar number call his phone. He ignored it and wouldn't have thought about it again if it hadn't immediately called right back, followed by a text. When he got up, answering it, everything he had been thinking was confirmed when he heard Shay say, "Get out! They coming!"

Chapter 99

Strip and Pooh had been listening to Mandy and Blacc's conversation on speakerphone, and they knew Blacc knew they were listening and what he meant when he said to come get the money. Running out of the room, they told Mandy to get downstairs to the truck, where Twist was waiting for her. Getting off the elevator on Mitch's floor, they were almost at Mitch's door when they heard gunshots.

Kicking in the door, they saw Blacc lying on the floor with a Mexican chick holding a towel to his chest. Stepping into the room, they saw a fat nigga lying against the bed, missing half of his head. On the floor, next to the bed, were bundles of money. Moving the fat nigga out of the way, they saw it had fallen from under the mattress. Lifting it, Pooh saw bundle after bundle of money. While Pooh was getting the money, Strip walked over to Blacc.

Blacc saw Strip approach and said, "I know I fucked up bad, bro, but hopefully, this makes up for some."

Strip nodded. "Maybe."

Blacc said, "If that didn't, this is Maria, our future plug. Take her with you and the money under the mattress, and give both of them to Memphis and Queen for me."

Strip looked at Blacc, confused. "Future plug?"

With blood coming out of his mouth, Blacc said, "Yeah, she don't speak no English, but all you gotta do is ask her who her brother is. Just make sure y'all take care of Mandy and the kids for me."

Looking at Maria, Blacc placed her hand in Strip's, saying in Spanish, "This one of my brothers. He about to introduce you to my family; they'll take good care of you," before closing his eyes for the last time…

Chapter 100

Despite what Queen told Shay, she was still sitting at the table, now smoking a blunt to the head while replaying everything that happened that day, as well as what Strip just called and told her. A lot of shit still didn't add up or make sense, the first thing being, where the fuck was her husband? With everything that had happened and taken place, there still hadn't been any word from him. The second was what to do with Mandy. If everything Strip said was true, she knew Memphis would honor Blacc's dying request, even if she didn't agree with the shit. Honestly, Memphis was softer and nicer than her. Three, who was this Mexican chick and her brother, and could they really open new doors for The Circle? Fourth, was the bullshit in the city really over, or did they still need to be looking over their shoulders? She was thinking about the fifth thing on her list when Strip, Pooh, and Twist walked in, followed by Maria and Mandy holding her kids.

Queen called Rosie while looking at Mandy. "It's been a long night. I had a room set up for you and the babies. Get some sleep, and we'll talk sometime tomorrow."

Looking at Maria, Queen had Strip translate, telling her that her name was Queen, and she was safe there. They had a room with a bathroom set up for her, and sometime tomorrow, they would take her shopping to buy her some clothes or whatever else she wanted and needed, and they had Rosie show her to her room as well. She looked at both Pooh and Strip, telling them to find a room and get some sleep.

Twist went to walk off, but Queen stopped her. "Say, what's up with you and ol' girl?"

Twist frowned. "Why? What you mean?"

Queen shook her head, really not feeling like going back and forth. "Bitch, where did she come from, and what was that shit at the restaurant about?"

Twist low-key had been wondering about the restaurant shit, too, and just put it off as Shay wanting to show her ass since she hadn't allowed her to cum, so she laughed. "Oh, she was just throwing a temper tantrum."

Queen shook her head. "Maybe, but what was up with Razor drawing on her?"

That was something else Twist had been wondering about and said, "Honestly, Queen, today been so crazy, I have no fuckin' idea!"

Queen looked at Twist. "It's a lot of uncertain shit going on concerning that bitch. In da morning, get rid of her."

Twist jumped up out of her seat. "Nawl, Queen, you tripping!"

Queen, fed up with all the events of the day, said, "Enjoy that bitch tonight, and like I said, tomorrow, get her ass out of here!"

Twist slapped the table, saying, "You ain't Memphis, and you don't run shit. You can't tell me who to fuck. Hell, if she gotta leave, I'm leaving too!"

Queen, remembering Twist questioning her authority earlier and the vow she made, laughed while pulling her locs up in a bun. She jumped around the table, catching Twist with a nasty two-piece that dropped her.

Twist yelled, "Bitch!"

Queen sat on Twist's chest, beating her ass, thinking about all the times Twist got slick.

Strip and Jimmy, hearing all the hollering, ran into the dining room, grabbing Queen off her. Jimmy was helping Twist up when Queen said, "Bitch, you got a choice. You can either get her the fuck out of here tomorrow, or I can bury both of y'all in these woods around here!"

Chapter 101

Besides the occasional smirks and giggles coming from Slim and TC, Dee somehow had a great time at breakfast, sitting and eating at IHOP with Kierra. Not only was she cute and funny, but she was also down-to-earth and smart, keeping the conversation going without acting weird when he ignored certain questions. Plus, she and Stacy hit it off immediately.

When they first arrived, Dee thought he was about to be the butt of all the jokes. Then, with pride and a silly, cute, sexy little dance and snap of her fingers, Kierra told the waitress to give her the all-you-can-eat pancakes special with eggs, sausage, and grits on the side.

Hearing Slim giggle, Dee was about to tell him to knock it off until Kierra came back with her own giggle, asking, "What's the problem, shoestring? You scared of not being able to shop in the little boys' section anymore?" making everybody laugh, especially Stacy, knowing that Slim's son, Tre, always complained that Slim stole his tank tops or wore his clothes.

TC was about to come back with his own joke until one look from Stacy shut it down, causing Kierra to laugh again, snapping her fingers. "Ohhwe, girl, I love the power of pussy!"

TC, not being able to refrain, mumbled, "Haha. You think yo' big ass so smart when I ain't even got no pussy yet."

Dee was about to say something when Stacy, out of nowhere, said, "And if you keep that attitude up, you ain't gon' be getting none either!"

Slim, who had just started drinking some water, laughed, spraying it all over his shirt and pants.

Getting to Kierra's house was a breeze, and she definitely got extra credit for it being clean and smelling good. She shocked the shit out of everybody when she said she bought it two years ago.

Dee, still trying to get back, asked, "You got it or bought it?" smirking.

Kierra said, "Nawl, smart ass, I bought it! Yeah, I got a small loan for it at first, but instead of letting them kill me with the interest and small payments, I said fuck it and sort of went broke for five whole months, paying it off in six months."

Everybody's mouths dropped. She went on to tell them that land in Iowa was cheap, especially around here. Stacy, listening to it all, made plans to talk to Memphis about it. It definitely seemed like something she could see herself doing.

Getting ready for bed, Kierra made the other room up while TC and Slim got the car from Arizona parked in the garage. Coming in, Slim saw a couple of blankets and pillows on the couch and stopped TC, who was about to walk past, by giving him one of each.

TC looked at them and then at Slim with a questioning look and could only smile when Slim said, "Look, I don't give a fuck what y'all do when I ain't around, but not under my watch!" causing them both to laugh.

Slim suspected he had been asleep for a couple of hours at most, but he was awakened by the loud screams and moans Kierra was making. Looking over, he saw the couch beside him was empty. Shaking his head, he got up, making it to the room Stacy was sleeping in. Cracking the door, he peeped in, seeing Stacy asleep under the covers with TC asleep on top of the covers, Stacy wrapped in his arms. Shaking his head again, Slim rolled a blunt and went on the porch to smoke it, thinking about his wife.

Chapter 102

Pooh heard the whole conversation, but he chose to stay out of it, as it wasn't his business or problem. On top of that, Pooh knew what Queen was saying was right. They didn't know enough about old girl to have her lying in their hideaway with them, with everything going on. It was already bad enough that the bitch was a witness to a murder he and his brother had committed by killing Skitz. That alone should have been enough for Twist to see the bitch had to go, especially when they'd all known Razor for most of their lives and had never seen him overreact. His upping his tool and aiming it at old girl said a lot: that they needed to get to the bottom of it sooner rather than later, which was why Pooh was there standing in the hallway when Jimmy and Twist bent the corner.

Twist, seeing Pooh, said, "You see what that bitch did to my face?"

Pooh shook his head. Her face was pretty fucked up. He said, "Yeah, but what would have happened if Memphis gave you an order, and you flat out said no and got smart?"

Twist, not liking that Pooh was taking Queen's side over hers, said, "But she ain't Memphis, and anyway, we all know that when Memphis make a order, he be done looked at it from every point of view. He don't demand some shit on impulse or because of his feelings toward it!"

Jimmy tried to intervene, but Pooh held his hand up, saying, "I got it, Unc." Looking at Twist, Pooh said, "You wrong. She basically is Memphis right now. Hell, that's his wife! Believe it or not, her law and word may be stronger than bro's, as he not gon' go against his wife unless it's something that he 110 percent for a fact know that she wrong on. Plus, again, what she saying makes sense for the good of The Circle, not just her. Shit, da girl saw me and Strip smoke somebody. What if the bitch run to them people or tell one day?"

Twist cut him off, shaking her head. "But she wouldn't do that!"

Pooh and Jimmy both looked at her. "But how you know? You ain't even known her twenty-four hours yet!"

Hearing this snapped Twist back to reality. So much had happened since she met Shay; she forgot it had only been that day, but it felt like months. Looking at Pooh, she said, "Damn, y'all right!" while shaking her head.

Dapping up Pooh, Twist turned to open her door and yelled, "Fuck!"

Pooh and Jimmy turned around, looking at Twist. "What's up?"

Twist pointed into the room at the open window and said, "She gone!"

Chapter 103

Strip had been sleeping for about an hour when he felt a presence on the bed with him. He was about to reach for his gun when he felt his dick getting squeezed. Slightly turning his head, the smell of alcohol hit his nose, instantly telling him who it was. Remembering what Pooh said, he was about to tell her no and put her out of his room until she went to bite his ear and suck on his neck, causing his dick to swell. Tired and not with all the foreplay, Strip rolled on top of her while pinning her down and began sucking on her titties because he had been thinking about it all day.

Hearing her panting turned him on even more, but he wasn't with the lovey dovey shit, as he knew this was only a one-time deal, so he let her arms down, preparing to pull her panties down, only to find out she wasn't wearing any. Feeling her warm and wet on his hands caused all thought to leave his big head, giving all power to the other one, which was exactly what he did. Not giving a damn if she was prepared for him or his size or not, he ran dead into her with a mission of punishing her for how she got smart and loud with him earlier.

Beating her insides up, he realized that today had been a very, very stressful day, so he took all of his frustrations out on her. Hearing her say 'cum in me' gave him pause until she said, 'it's okay. I had my uterus taken out,' causing him to pound her extra hard. Going as deep as he could in her, he busted long and hard with them both falling asleep like that.

He was brought out of his sleep by the cocking of a gun. Sitting up made Toya do the same, and they were both shocked to see Queen sitting in a chair at the foot of the bed, holding a gun. Toya, seeing that Strip didn't know what to say, asked, "Ummm, Pumpkin, what the fuck is you doing?" When Queen didn't respond, Toya got louder, saying, "Girl, I know you heard me. What the fuck are you doing, just sitting there, holding a gun at that?"

Queen shook her head, looking at her mama, and gave Strip a disappointed look. "If I didn't love both of y'all, I'd kill y'all right here, right now."

Strip, seeing the seriousness on her face, didn't respond, but Toya, still not knowing her daughter, said, "Bitch, what?"

Queen looked at her mother and said, "I love you, Mama, and I know you don't really know what's goin' on, but please don't make me show and prove to you just who the fuck I am."

Toya, not liking the way her daughter was talking to her, screwed her face up, about to come back with her own slick shit until Strip, feeling her tense up, put his palms out to her and shook his head.

Getting up, Queen looked at Strip. "Get dressed, and meet me at the table ASAP. I gotta talk to you about a few things."

Looking at her mother, she tossed her the phone she allowed Shay to use last night and said, "Never overstep what the fuck I say again."

Toya looked at the phone. "What?"

Shaking her head, Queen said, "When you check the text messages, you'll see," before stepping out of the room. She then looked at both. "This was a one-time thing. I don't want to hear shit else about this."

Strip looked at Queen. "I got you, sis."

Queen shook her head. "No, you don't, or this would've never happened," before closing the door behind her.

Chapter 104

Rosie, Bailey, and Key got up early after getting a good night's sleep, only to go downstairs hungry to see that there was nothing to eat. Agreeing to cook breakfast for everyone, they decided to go to the grocery store. Remembering yesterday, Bailey ran back into her and Pooh's room, grabbing one of Pooh's guns.

After making sure they had enough food for everyone, they were walking to the register when Bailey kept seeing people glance and sometimes stare at her. Walking past the magazines and newspapers, she was surprised to see her face on the front page, saying she was wanted for questioning in over two dozen murders. Not wanting to make any fast or sudden moves to draw more attention to herself, she asked Key for her keys, saying she wasn't feeling well.

Rosie and Key came out, pushing the basket, joking that Bailey might possibly be pregnant. Getting in the truck, they were all joking as they pulled out when Bailey noticed two police cars with their sirens on, speeding up to the store.

Her thoughts were interrupted by Key looking at her crazily. "I know that's your friend, but damn."

Bailey looked at her confusedly, asking, "What?"

Key looked at her. "Me and Rosie was just talking, and we wonder what Memphis or Queen gon' decide to do about Mandy!"

Bailey shook her head, saying, "I don't know!" wondering what she was going to do her damn self. Pulling back up, they were taking all the bags of groceries into the kitchen when Ms. Rhonda walked in, seeing Bailey, and snapped. "What the fuck is she doing here?"

Key and Rosie looked at each other, then at Bailey, before asking Ms. Rhonda what she was talking about.

Ms. Rhonda, in a loud voice, said, "I told that lil' bitch and my grandson that I didn't wanna see any of their faces until everybody that had something to do with my daughter being hurt was dead!"

Key and Rosie's mouths fell open.

Bailey, sick and tired of being talked to like she wasn't part of this family, said, "They are, bitch! Go check the news!" before storming out of the kitchen to find Pooh.

Chapter 105

Queen had been up all night and early morning, literally going through a whole pack of Dutches, just blowing and thinking. Jimmy bringing her Toya's phone wasn't bad at first, as she was low-key glad to hear that the lil' bitch was gone and out of their hair. All that changed at about a quarter to six when, out of boredom, she called her house, checking the answering machine, and accidentally clicked the envelope button instead of 'end' on her mom's Android.

Seeing a message being sent a few hours ago caught her attention: one, because everyone knew the rules about texting, and second, because she'd had the phone for over an hour. Seeing the words 'This Shay. Get out. They coming,' first, it confused the fuck out of her, then made her blood boil as she put two and two together, which, in turn, made a few more of the puzzle pieces fall into place.

It honestly wanted to make her go wake Twist up and beat her ass again. Thinking outside the box, though, like Memphis always preached to her, she knew that would do no good. Plus, they had a visit with Bronze set up in a couple of hours, and she knew Twist's face couldn't be too fucked up, or they would never let them in. Counting the money that Pooh gave her last night put them at just under $400,000, including the money Slim called less than an hour ago to tell her they had, as well as giving an update on where they were and everything that happened.

Smoking her last blunt, she opened her browser, about to try logging into Memphis's Facebook account, seeing that she knew all his passwords. Then Bailey's face suddenly popped up on her screen, saying that she was wanted for questioning in over two dozen murders. Surprisingly, none of the boys' faces, nor her,s were on there. So far, they were just looking for Bailey.

Wanting another ear to bounce a few things off of, she went to wake Strip up, only to find her mother snuggled up on him in the bed. She could tell by how the bed was that they had fucked, which honestly didn't matter or bother her, as she didn't give a fuck who or what her mom fucked. It was the point that not only had she endangered them by giving the bitch Shay her phone after she said no, but she was fucking someone in The Circle that was already family, which was just nasty in her eyes.

Plus, she had been around all the guys long enough to know how they talked, and she didn't want or need her mother to be the topic of one of their conversations, especially now, with everything going on. Not to mention, for years now, her mom had been talking shit to her for marrying and fucking with Memphis, only for her to fuck on his older brother, which was basically the same thing to her, if not worse. Her only problem with Strip was that she thought they had way more love and respect between them for him ever to do something like that.

I mean, shit, if they were brother and sister, and that was her mom, that meant she was his too, right? Her thoughts were interrupted by yelling coming from the kitchen area. Getting close, she heard Ms. Rhonda's words and was about to speak up for Bailey until, for once, the white girl let her nuts hang, telling Ms. Rhonda how it was.

Queen smiled, thinking today may just be a good day. Walking back into the dining room, she saw Strip already sitting there. She was about to send Rosie to get Pooh and Twist when Twist walked in with her head down. She smirked, seeing the humbleness Twist was showing, she and knew it would only progress once she saw or heard about the text message.

Pooh came in last, saying, "Sis, we gotta talk."

Queen nodded. "I think I already know what it's about, but you can have the floor as soon as I get through telling y'all where we at right now."

Pooh nodded, saying, "Bet."

Queen said, "First, I still ain't heard from y'all brother yet, and at this point, I'm starting to think some foul shit. Second, me and Twist got a visit with Bronze in about an hour. He said it's an emergency, and y'all niggas know that nigga don't even talk like that. Third, I need y'all to get ready to head to Des Moines, Iowa, first and then on to North Dakota."

Both boys looked at each other with one saying, "Iowa?" and the other saying, "North Dakota?"

Queen said, "Yeah, a lot of shit happened out that way yesterday."

Before they could say anything else, Lil' Pooh ran into the room, saying. "Dad, Mom say where aunty Stacy at?"

They both said Stacy's name while looking at Queen. She looked at both of them, answering their question by nodding her head. Speaking up, Queen said, "Yesterday, the nigga y'all brother sent her to meet tried robbing and kidnapping her."

Before Queen could say another word, both boys were out of their seats, moving in different directions with the same goal in mind: get to Stacy and whoever the fuck tried their little sister.

Chapter 106

Shay made it out of the cabin just in time. Even jumping out of the window had been a bitch, due to her shoulder. Walking around the back of the cabin, she saw Strip, Pooh, and Twist getting out of the truck with a couple more people with them, which couldn't be good for her unless Mitch made it out in time, which she was hoping, as she didn't know how she or her family could go on living without the baby of the family there to brighten up their day.

Getting out of Scottsdale had been a breeze because as soon as she got on the main road, an older white guy immediately picked her up, trying to trick with her. Of course, she flirted and played along, even rubbing on his little dick through his cargo shorts, until he got out at the store, supposedly grabbing some condoms and a Red Bull. The second he had walked into the store, she hopped in the driver's seat and took off.

Heading back to South Phoenix, she almost had a panic attack, thinking about going home and admitting defeat to her family. Of course, Mikey's tricking ass wouldn't answer his phone at this time of morning, probably out of fear it was a bitch calling for some dick and money while he was laid up with one he was giving both dick and money to. Saying fuck it, she knew who would help her at any and every cost if nobody else would.

Pulling up in front of her uncle Skitz's house felt weird as hell to her, knowing he would never be able to walk out of the house, Crip-walking like he was so famous for doing. Nor would they be having family functions there anymore, like he was always throwing. Getting out of the car, she wiped her eyes, trying to dry them, not wanting to appear weak around her little cousin Cory, as she knew he hated weakness with a passion.

As she went up the walkway, a yellow-skinned nigga with braids tried stopping her and even tried getting hostile with her when she ignored his advances. She had just gotten a couple of knocks on the door when the young nigga grabbed her arm, pulling her back down the stairs. The nigga drew back to slap her when Cory's voice boomed off the porch.

"Bitch nigga, if you do, that'll be the last motherfucka you ever slap in yo' life."

Snatching away from the nigga, Shay couldn't help it and broke down crying, screaming, "They killed him! They killed Uncle Skitz!"

Cory, with a scowl on his face, snatched Shay in his arms, asking, "Who? Who did?"

Hearing Shay say it was Strip and Pooh caused Cory to drop to his knees, swearing on the set. He vowed to kill everybody in The Circle.

Chapter 107

Before leaving the cabin, going to see Bronze, Queen gave Jimmy the $50,000 back he spent renting the Airbnb, telling him to hold the deposit for them in case they needed it later to invest in something. She also gave Rosie $10,000, telling her to go around and get everyone's sizes and a list of anything else anybody may need, as well as stocking up on things they needed at the cabin, before stopping at the house to get Diamond.

On the way to the jail, she had Twist stop and get a new phone, prepaying it for six months, and folded a stack of hundred-dollar bills around it for Bronze.

Walking in, the girl saw Twist putting the phone with the money in the drop spot and said, "My name Alicia. I'ma give you my number before you leave. It's a lot more I can do for y'all besides just this."

Queen, hearing it, nodded. "It's a lot that comes with fuckin' with us. Are you sure you ready for all that?"

Alicia licked her lips, looking at the money, and said. "I'm down for anything if y'all paying like this. Hell, I may even be willing to give Bronze some pussy with y'all paying like this."

Queen said, "When you give her your number, write yo' CashApp down, and the bread will be there tonight. But if you accept my money, you better make sure my brother have a good time!"

Laughing, walking away, Alicia said, "It'll be my pleasure!"

Walking into the visitation room, Bronze was aware of the stares and mugs coming his way.

Feeling the tension, Twist asked him, "What the fuck is everybody problem?"

Shaking his head, Bronze said, "No disrespect, Queen, but you motherfuckas done started World War III out there and got it hard for these niggas to eat in here!"

Queen looked Bronze in his eyes and said, "Since when do wolves give a fuck what sheep think? Motherfuckas touched ours, so everybody had to feel it. Hell, I ain't saying what Pooh did was right, but I ain't saying what he did was wrong either." Raising her voice so she could be heard, Queen continued. "The Circle gives respect to receive respect. We don't give a fuck who it is. If a motherfucka step out of line, they will get smashed."

Hearing her words, Bronze could only agree with her, but he lowered his voice. "Yeah, but what's up with that Skitz shit? You know that nigga was real reputable out here and Cali. We got away with shooting him and shit because everybody knew he crossed the line. But word on the streets is, we exed 'em out when he came to us on some peaceful, respectful, business-type shit. Not to mention, that nigga Razor had a lot of love both out there and in here. Plus, he rode heavy for us."

Queen looked at Twist, causing her to drop her head, and said, "Yeah, I know. It's a lot of shit that motherfuckas gon' talk about that they don't know about."

Bronze said, "Yeah, but all this rumor shit coming from they niece! She said she was there!"

Queen and Twist looked at each other, saying, *"Their niece?"*

Bronze nodded his head, saying, "Yeah, Shay is Skit's sister's third-oldest daughter! Skit's sister's second-oldest daughter, Carla, is Razor's daughter!"

Shaking her head, Twist said, "Damn, how many daughters do the bitch got?"

Laughing, Bronze said, "Four! Which is crazy because her youngest daughter's baby daddy, Mitch, was found slumped this morning in Mesa with another nigga!"

Twist and Queen stared at each other again.

The rest of the visit was just a recap of Bronze telling them all he heard on inmate.com and shit he had then been through, as well as shit he was overhearing motherfuckas talk about, Twist filling in a few blanks for him until he brought up the situation with his lawyer. Queen told him she'd make sure his lawyer had the bread by the end of the day, which really surprised Bronze.

Bringing up the situation with Ace caused Queen to look at Twist questioningly, as she had personally counted the money for Ace before giving it to Memphis to drop off at Twist's house, so to hear that Ace hadn't been paid was confusing as fuck.

Frowning, Twist said, "Hold up, wait. What you mean, he ain't been paid? I gave that money to Blacc a couple weeks ago!"

Mugging Twist, Bronze said, "If that's the case, you know the procedure. Why the fuck didn't you tell Memphis or Queen when you didn't hear from Ace within forty-eight hours of him supposedly getting his money?"

Twist shook her head. "Honestly, with everything Memphis had going on, I didn't want to bother him if it was simply a mistake or overlook."

Bronze said, "Yeah, and if it wasn't for the nail in the horse's hoof, the war would've been won too," referring to the four bodies, causing Twist to drop her head.

That pissed Bronze off more. "Nigga, I don't know who fucked up yo' face like that, but they shoulda beat some sense into you!"

With visitation about to end, Bronze gave Queen Ace's number, saying, "He needs to be called today, sis!"

Before walking out, Queen promised him she would before saying, "I hope you like yo' lil' surprise!" while smirking.

Getting in the truck, Queen dialed Ace's number, waiting for Twist to get the DO chick Alicia's number and CashApp info. Hearing someone answer, Queen explained who she was before confirming who she was speaking with.

Getting Ace, Queen said, "Sorry it was a missed payment. We've been clearing house, as there was some sort of in-house fraud going on. Now that everything's been straightened out, we would love to make good on our payment and obligation."

Laughing, and in a strange accent, Ace said, "I'm sure. As long as you do understand that some interest fees been added on."

Agreeing, Queen said, "That's not a problem. Just let me know the price tag, and I'll do my best to get that to you immediately."

Laughing again, Ace said, "Eight hundred with a K behind it!"

Frowning, as Queen knew she wasn't the best counter in the world, but first, she didn't understand how the 300K she knew they owed—because she had counted—had more than doubled. Second, even if he did double it to 600K, which she could understand and respect, where did the extra 200K come from?

"Umm, I understand that we're on the horn, but where did the extra 200K come from, even if the bill had been double?" she asked and was confused by his answer.

Ace said, "For making him set an example!"

Confused, Queen asked, "What? What do you mean?"

Laughing, Ace said, "Setting an example. You know, letting y'all know y'all could be touched," before hanging up the phone.

Chapter 108

Rosie and Jimmy were tired from running around shopping all morning. Leaving the hospital after spending time with Whitney and giving Butch a small but much-needed break, they stopped at the house so they could get Diamond and so Rosie could grab a few things Queen told her to.

Walking around the quiet house, Rosie shook her head, as it honestly felt weird and foreign to her. Never had the house felt so cold and lonely, so even when she picked up the phone, attempting to forward it to the number Queen had given her, and she didn't hear a dial tone, she thought it was one more weird thing to add to the list until she heard a nigga hiss, "About fuckin' time!"

Rosie, confused, said, "Huh?"

In an angry voice, the nigga said, "Bitch, you hear me. How much do you love yo' husband?"

Laughing, Rosie said, "Ohh, you must think I'm my sister, but you don't have to be mean or rude. She not here right now. Do you wanna leave a message?"

Pissed off, the nigga said, "Put somebody else on the phone!"

Shrugging, Rosie handed Jimmy the phone. "I guess they want you."

Confused, Jimmy grabbed the phone, saying, "Hello?"

The nigga said, "Listen closely because I ain't about to keep playing phone tag. If you want to see Memphis and the lil' girl alive again, I want a million for the lil' girl and two million for Memphis. I know it may take y'all broke ass a lil' time to get that money up, so I'll call again in seventy-two hours with the instructions of where to take it."

Jimmy was asking, "What lil' girl?" when the phone hung up.

Chapter 109

Strip, Pooh, and Bailey had been on the road for about three hours before Strip remembered he planned to holler at Queen. Picking up the phone, hitting her number, he was about to hang up, thinking she was busy, but she finally answered.

Hearing her voice, he said, "Hey, I almost forgot. I left a tape on top of the nightstand in the room I was in that I need you and Jimmy to check out."

When she didn't respond, he said, "Hey, sis, did you hear me?"

Queen said, "Yeah, a tape."

Strip, sensing something wasn't right, said, "What's up, sis? What's wrong?"

With her voice cracking, she said, "I know where yo' brother at."

Strip said, "That's a good thing then! What's wrong?"

Queen started crying. "He's been kidnapped! They want $3 million for him!"

Three million? Strip thought. *What they really want is to die!*

To be continued...

Lock Down Publications and Ca$h Presents
Assisted Publishing Packages

Due to an increase in the price of services we have increased our prices. The prices below reflect the price increase as of 11/1/24.

BASIC PACKAGE	UPGRADED PACKAGE
$699	**$1000**
Editing	Typing
Cover Design	Editing
Formatting	Cover Design
	Formatting
	Upload eBooks to Amazon
	Upload Paperback to Amazon
ADVANCE PACKAGE	**LDP SUPREME PACKAGE**
$1,400	**$1,700**
Typing	Typing
Editing (line editing/content)	Editing (line editing/content)
Cover Design	Cover Design
Formatting	Formatting
Copyright Registration	Copyright Registration
Proofreading	Proofreading
Upload eBooks to Amazon	Set up Amazon Account
Upload Paperback to Amazon	Upload eBooks to Amazon
	Upload Paperback to Amazon
	Advertise on LDP's Amazon and Facebook Page

***

Other services available upon request.
Additional charges may apply

Lock Down Publications
P.O. Box 944
Stockbridge, GA 30281-9998
Phone: 470 303-9761
Email: lockdownpublications@gmail.com

228

Submission Guideline

Submit the first three chapters of your completed manuscript to ldpsubmissions@gmail.com. In the subject line add **Your Book's Title**. The manuscript must be in a Word Doc file and sent as an attachment. Document should be in Times New Roman, double spaced, and in size 12 font. Also, provide your synopsis and full contact information. If sending multiple submissions, they must each be in a separate email.

Have a story but no way to send it electronically? You can still submit to LDP/Ca$h Presents. Send in the first three chapters, written or typed, of your completed manuscript to:

LDP: Submissions Dept
P.O. Box 944
Stockbridge, GA 30281-9998

DO NOT send original manuscript. Must be a duplicate. Provide your synopsis and a cover letter containing your full contact information.

Thanks for considering LDP and Ca$h Presents.

NEW RELEASES

BLOODLINE OF A SAVAGE 1-3
THESE VICIOUS STREETS 1-3
RELENTLESS GOON 1-3
BY PRINCE A. TAUHID

THE BUTTERFLY MAFIA 1-3
BY FUMIYA PAYNE

A THUG'S STREET PRINCESS 1&2
BY MEESHA

CITY OF SMOKE 3
BY MOLOTTI

GET IT IN SLUGS 1 &2
BY B. STALL

STANDING ON HER BUSINESS 1&2
BY DG SANTANA

STEPPERS 1,2&3
THE REAL BADDIES OF CHI-RAQ
BY KING RIO

THE LANE 1&2
BY KEN-KEN SPENCE

THUG OF SPADES 1&2
LOVE IN THE TRENCHES 2
CORNER BOYS
BY COREY ROBINSON

TIL DEATH 3
BY ARYANNA

SAVAGE DREAMZ | KING DAVID

THE BIRTH OF A GANGSTER 4
BY DELMONT PLAYER

PRODUCT OF THE STREETS 1-3
BY DEMOND "MONEY" ANDERSON

NO TIME FOR ERROR
BY KEESE

MONEY HUNGRY DEMONS 1-2
BY TRANAY ADAMS

HUB CITY MENACE 1-3
BY J. WHITE

A THUGGISH PASSION 1&2
LAND OF DA HOOLIGANZ 1-4
KILLAZ ON STANDBY 1&2
BY IRA B.

FO'EVA ROLLIN 1&2
BY ASSA RAYMOND BAKER

THE LEVEL UP 1&3
BY LUXURY KING

Coming Soon from Lock Down Publications/Ca$h Presents

IF YOU CROSS ME ONCE 6
ANGEL V
By Anthony Fields

A THUGS STREET PRINCESS 3
By Meesha

CORNER BOYS 2
By Corey Robinson

THA TAKEOVER
By Keith Chandler

BETRAYAL OF A G 2
By Ray Vinci

SAVAGE FAMILY EMPIRE 1&2
SOULLESS GOON 1,2&3
THE DIRTY SIDE OF MONEY 1,2&3
By Prince

FOR MY ENEMY'S SAKE
AMBITIONS OF A SLIDER
FRESH OFF DA PORCH
By IRA B.

BY THE TRUCKLOAD 1-4
TIPPIN' THE SCALES 1-3
BAD BITCHES WIT GUNZ 3
PROBLEM SOLVED 2
By Christopher "Diesel" Hornezes

Available Now

RESTRAINING ORDER 1 & 2
By **CA$H & Coffee**

LOVE KNOWS NO BOUNDARIES 1-3
By **Coffee**

RAISED AS A GOON I, II, III & IV
BRED BY THE SLUMS I, II, III
BLAST FOR ME I & II
ROTTEN TO THE CORE I II III
A BRONX TALE I, II, III
DUFFLE BAG CARTEL I II III IV V VI
HEARTLESS GOON I II III IV V
A SAVAGE DOPEBOY I II
DRUG LORDS I II III
CUTTHROAT MAFIA I II
KING OF THE TRENCHES
By **Ghost**

LAY IT DOWN I & II
LAST OF A DYING BREED I II
BLOOD STAINS OF A SHOTTA I & II III
By **Jamaica**

LOYAL TO THE GAME I II III
LIFE OF SIN I, II III
By **TJ & Jelissa**

IF LOVING HIM IS WRONG…I & II
LOVE ME EVEN WHEN IT HURTS I II III
By **Jelissa**

PUSH IT TO THE LIMIT
By **Bre' Hayes**

SAVAGE DREAMZ | KING DAVID

BLOODY COMMAS I & II
SKI MASK CARTEL I, II & III
KING OF NEW YORK I II, III IV V
RISE TO POWER I II III
COKE KINGS I II III IV V
BORN HEARTLESS I II III IV
KING OF THE TRAP I II
By **T.J. Edwards**

WHEN THE STREETS CLAP BACK I & II III
THE HEART OF A SAVAGE I II III IV
MONEY MAFIA I II
LOYAL TO THE SOIL I II III
By **Jibril Williams**

A DISTINGUISHED THUG STOLE MY HEART I II & III
LOVE SHOULDN'T HURT I II III IV
RENEGADE BOYS 1-4
PAID IN KARMA 1-3
SAVAGE STORMS 1-3
AN UNFORESEEN LOVE 1-3
BABY, I'M WINTERTIME COLD 1-3
A THUG'S STREET PRINCESS 1&2
By **Meesha**

A GANGSTER'S CODE 1-3
A GANGSTER'S SYN 1-3
THE SAVAGE LIFE 1-3
CHAINED TO THE STREETS 1-3
BLOOD ON THE MONEY 1-3
A GANGSTA'S PAIN 1-3
BEAUTIFUL LIES AND UGLY TRUTHS
CHURCH IN THESE STREETS
By **J-Blunt**

CUM FOR ME 1-8
An LDP Erotica Collaboration

SAVAGE DREAMZ | KING DAVID

BLOOD OF A BOSS 1-5
SHADOWS OF THE GAME
TRAP BASTARD
By **Askari**

THE STREETS BLEED MURDER 1-3
THE HEART OF A GANGSTA 1-3
By **Jerry Jackson**

WHEN A GOOD GIRL GOES BAD
By **Adrienne**

THE COST OF LOYALTY 1-3
By **Kweli**

BRIDE OF A HUSTLA 1-3
THE FETTI GIRLS 1-3
CORRUPTED BY A GANGSTA 1-4
BLINDED BY HIS LOVE
THE PRICE YOU PAY FOR LOVE 1-3
DOPE GIRL MAGIC 1-3
By **Destiny Skai**

A KINGPIN'S AMBITION
A KINGPIN'S AMBITION II
I MURDER FOR THE DOUGH
By **Ambitious**

TRUE SAVAGE 1-7
DOPE BOY MAGIC 1-3
MIDNIGHT CARTEL 1-3
CITY OF KINGZ 1&2
NIGHTMARE ON SILENT AVE
THE PLUG OF LIL MEXICO 1&2
CLASSIC CITY
By **Chris Green**

SAVAGE DREAMZ | KING DAVID

A GANGSTER'S REVENGE 1-4
THE BOSS MAN'S DAUGHTERS 1-5
A SAVAGE LOVE 1&2
BAE BELONGS TO ME 1&2
A HUSTLER'S DECEIT 1-3
WHAT BAD BITCHES DO 1-3
SOUL OF A MONSTER 1-3
KILL ZONE
A DOPE BOY'S QUEEN 1-3
TIL DEATH 1-3
IMMA DIE BOUT MINE 1-6
DYING FOR LIKES
By **Aryanna**

A DOPEBOY'S PRAYER
By **Eddie "Wolf" Lee**

THE KING CARTEL 1-3
By **Frank Gresham**

THESE NIGGAS AIN'T LOYAL 1-3
By **Nikki Tee**

GANGSTA SHYT 1-3
By **CATO**

THE ULTIMATE BETRAYAL
By **Phoenix**

BOSS'N UP 1-3
By **Royal Nicole**

I LOVE YOU TO DEATH
By **Destiny J**

I RIDE FOR MY HITTA
I STILL RIDE FOR MY HITTA
By **Misty Holt**

LOVE & CHASIN' PAPER
By **Qay Crockett**

TO DIE IN VAIN
SINS OF A HUSTLA
By **ASAD**

BROOKLYN HUSTLAZ
By **Boogsy Morina**

BROOKLYN ON LOCK 1 & 2
By **Sonovia**

GANGSTA CITY
By **Teddy Duke**

A DRUG KING AND HIS DIAMOND 1-3
A DOPEMAN'S RICHES
HER MAN, MINE'S TOO 1&2
CASH MONEY HO'S
THE WIFEY I USED TO BE 1&2
PRETTY GIRLS DO NASTY THINGS
By **Nicole Goosby**

LIPSTICK KILLAH 1-3
CRIME OF PASSION 1-3
FRIEND OR FOE 1-3
By **Mimi**

TRAPHOUSE KING 1-3
KINGPIN KILLAZ 1-3
STREET KINGS 1&2
PAID IN BLOOD 1&2
CARTEL KILLAZ 1-3
DOPE GODS 1&2
By **Hood Rich**

THE STREETS ARE CALLING
By **Duquie Wilson**

STEADY MOBBN' 1-3
THE STREETS STAINED MY SOUL 1-3
By **Marcellus Allen**

WHO SHOT YA 1-3
SON OF A DOPE FIEND 1-4
HEAVEN GOT A GHETTO 1&2
SKI MASK MONEY 1&2
By **Renta**

GORILLAZ IN THE BAY 1-4
TEARS OF A GANGSTA 1/&2
3X KRAZY 1&2
STRAIGHT BEAST MODE 1&2
By **DE'KARI**

TRIGGADALE 1-3
MURDA WAS THE CASE 1-3
By **Elijah R. Freeman**

SLAUGHTER GANG 1-3
RUTHLESS HEART 1-3
By **Willie Slaughter**

GOD BLESS THE TRAPPERS 1-3
THESE SCANDALOUS STREETS 1-3
FEAR MY GANGSTA 1-5
THESE STREETS DON'T LOVE NOBODY 1-2
BURY ME A G 1-5
A GANGSTA'S EMPIRE 1-4
THE DOPEMAN'S BODYGAURD 1&2
THE REALEST KILLAZ 1-3
THE LAST OF THE OGS 1-3
By **Tranay Adams**

MARRIED TO A BOSS 1-3
By **Destiny Skai & Chris Green**

KINGZ OF THE GAME 1-7
CRIME BOSS 1-4
By **Playa Ray**

FUK SHYT
By **Blakk Diamond**

DON'T F#CK WITH MY HEART 1&2
By **Linnea**

ADDICTED TO THE DRAMA 1-3
IN THE ARM OF HIS BOSS
By **Jamila**

LOYALTY AIN'T PROMISED 1&2
By **Keith Williams**

YAYO 1-4
A SHOOTER'S AMBITION 1&2
BRED IN THE GAME
By **S. Allen**

TRAP GOD 1-3
RICH $AVAGE 1-3
MONEY IN THE GRAVE 1-3
CARTEL MONEY 1&2
By **Martell Troublesome Bolden**

FOREVER GANGSTA 1&2
GLOCKS ON SATIN SHEETS 1&2
By **Adrian Dulan**

TOE TAGZ 1-4
LEVELS TO THIS SHYT 1&2
IT'S JUST ME AND YOU
By **Ah'Million**

SAVAGE DREAMZ | KING DAVID

KINGPIN DREAMS 1-3
RAN OFF ON DA PLUG
By **Paper Boi Rari**

THE STREETS MADE ME 1-3
By **Larry D. Wright**

CONFESSIONS OF A GANGSTA 1-4
CONFESSIONS OF A JACKBOY 1-3
CONFESSIONS OF A HITMAN
CONFESSIONS OF A DOPE BOY
By **Nicholas Lock**

I'M NOTHING WITHOUT HIS LOVE
SINS OF A THUG
TO THE THUG I LOVED BEFORE
A GANGSTA SAVED XMAS
IN A HUSTLER I TRUST
By **Monet Dragun**

QUIET MONEY 1-3
THUG LIFE 1-3
EXTENDED CLIP 1&2
A GANGSTA'S PARADISE
By **Trai'Quan**

CAUGHT UP IN THE LIFE 1-3
THE STREETS NEVER LET GO 1-3
By **Robert Baptiste**

NEW TO THE GAME 1-3
MONEY, MURDER & MEMORIES 1-3
By **Malik D. Rice**

CREAM 2-3
THE STREETS WILL TALK
By **Yolanda Moore**

SAVAGE DREAMZ | KING DAVID

THE STREETS WILL NEVER CLOSE 1-3
By **K'ajji**

LIFE OF A SAVAGE 1-4
A GANGSTA'S QUR'AN 1-4
MURDA SEASON 1-3
GANGLAND CARTEL 1-3
CHI'RAQ GANGSTAS 1-4
KILLERS ON ELM STREET 1-3
JACK BOYZ N DA BRONX 1-3
A DOPEBOY'S DREAM 1-3
JACK BOYS VS DOPE BOYS 1-3
COKE GIRLZ
COKE BOYS
SOSA GANG 1&2
BRONX SAVAGES
BODYMORE KINGPINS
BLOOD OF A GOON
By **Romell Tukes**

CONCRETE KILLA 1-3
VICIOUS LOYALTY 1-3
BLOODY MONEY BAGS
By **Kingpen**

THE ULTIMATE SACRIFICE 1-6
KHADIFI
IF YOU CROSS ME ONCE 1-3
ANGEL 1-4
IN THE BLINK OF AN EYE
By **Anthony Fields**

THE LIFE OF A HOOD STAR
By **Ca$h & Rashia Wilson**

NIGHTMARES OF A HUSTLA 1-3
BLOOD AND GAMES 1&2
By **King Dream**

GHOST MOB
By **Stilloan Robinson**

HARD AND RUTHLESS 1&2
MOB TOWN 251
THE BILLIONAIRE BENTLEYS 1-3
REAL G'S MOVE IN SILENCE
By **Von Diesel**

MOB TIES 1-7
SOUL OF A HUSTLER, HEART OF A KILLER 1-3
GORILLAZ IN THE TRENCHES
OOPS CRY TOO 1&2
THE DAUGHTER OF A CARTEL BOSS
By **SayNoMore**

BODYMORE MURDERLAND 1-3
THE BIRTH OF A GANGSTER 1-4
By **Delmont Player**

FOR THE LOVE OF A BOSS 1&2
By **C. D. Blue**

KILLA KOUNTY 1-5
TENDER
By **Khufu**

MOBBED UP 1-4
THE BRICK MAN 1-5
THE COCAINE PRINCESS 1-10
STEPPERS 1-3
SUPER GREMLIN 1-4
A GANGSTA'S SON
By **King Rio**

MONEY GAME 1&2
By **Smoove Dolla**

SAVAGE DREAMZ | KING DAVID

A GANGSTA'S KARMA 1-5
By **FLAME**

KING OF THE TRENCHES 1-3
By **GHOST & TRANAY ADAMS**

BAD BITCHES WIT GUNZ 1&2
PROBLEM SOLVED
By **"Christopher Diesel" Hornezes**

QUEEN OF THE ZOO 1&2
By **Black Migo**

GRIMEY WAYS 1-3
BETRAYAL OF A G
By **Ray Vinci**

XMAS WITH AN ATL SHOOTER
By **Ca$h & Destiny Skai**

KING KILLA 1&2
By **Vincent "Vitto" Holloway**

BETRAYAL OF A THUG 1&2
By **Fre$h**

COUNTDOWN OF A KILLA 1&2
SEX, MURDER AND GOD 1&2
GUNS DOWN, BOTTOMS UP 1&2
By Lo-Life

THE MURDER QUEENS 1-7
By **Michael Gallon**

FOR THE LOVE OF BLOOD 1-4
By **Jamel Mitchell**

SAVAGE DREAMZ | KING DAVID

HOOD CONSIGLIERE 1&2
NO TIME FOR ERROR
By **Keese**

PROTÉGÉ OF A LEGEND 1,2&3
LOVE IN THE TRENCHES 1&2
By **Corey Robinson**

THE PLUG'S RUTHLESS DAUGHTER 1&2
By **Tony Daniels**

BORN IN THE GRAVE 1-3
CRIME PAYS
By **Self Made Tay**

MOAN IN MY MOUTH
By **XTASY**

TORN BETWEEN A GANGSTER AND A GENTLEMAN
By **J-BLUNT & Miss Kim**

LOYALTY IS EVERYTHING 1-3
CITY OF SMOKE 1-3
By **Molotti**

HERE TODAY GONE TOMORROW 1&2
By **Fly Rock**

WOMEN LIE MEN LIE 1-4
FIFTY SHADES OF SNOW 1-3
STACK BEFORE YOU SPLURGE
GIRLS FALL LIKE DOMINOES
NAÏVE TO THE STREETS
By **ROY MILLIGAN**

PILLOW PRINCESS
By **S. Hawkins**

SAVAGE DREAMZ | KING DAVID

THE BUTTERFLY MAFIA 1-3
SALUTE MY SAVAGERY 1&2
By **Fumiya Payne**

THE LANE 1&2
By Ken-Ken Spence

THE PUSSY TRAP 1-5
By **Nene Capri**

DIRTY DNA
By **Blaque**

SANCTIFIED AND HORNY
by **XTASY**

BOOKS BY LDP'S CEO, CA$H

TRUST IN NO MAN
TRUST IN NO MAN 2
TRUST IN NO MAN 3
BONDED BY BLOOD
SHORTY GOT A THUG
THUGS CRY
THUGS CRY 2
THUGS CRY 3
TRUST NO BITCH
TRUST NO BITCH 2
TRUST NO BITCH 3
TIL MY CASKET DROPS
RESTRAINING ORDER
RESTRAINING ORDER 2
IN LOVE WITH A CONVICT
LIFE OF A HOOD STAR
XMAS WITH AN ATL SHOOTER